New
Voices
Playwrights
Theatre

Annual Anthology of Short Plays

2020

Edited by

John Bolen

New Voices Playwrights Theatre
a 501(c)(3) corporation
P.O.Box 53921, Irvine, CA 92619-3921
newvoicesplaywrights.org
newvoicesplaywrights@gmail.com

Table of Contents

Foreword

At the time of this writing, the corona-virus pandemic has swept the world, causing the governor of California to order the closure of all non-essential businesses in the state. He has also ordered that all citizens of the state self quarantine at home. This has resulted in the closure of all theatrical productions, throwing actors, directors and tech people out of work. There are similar orders across the USA, so this collaborative art form has come to a halt throughout the land and the world. The immenseness of these actions to stop the spread of the virus has had no match since World War II.

However, as discussed in previous forewords to this series of anthologies, plays, although collaborative in achieving a full production, are by themselves stand alone literature. The readers of plays, like the readers of any form of literature, when once attuned to the eccentricities of the form, can find themselves drawn into the whole world of ideas that the playwright wishes to convey.

In theatres around the world, when all is shut down, the actors have gone home; the overhead lights have gone dark; and there is a single bulb atop a floor lamp that is left to shine - the ghost light. To some, it is simply obeying an Equity safety rule, where there are so many things that may harm someone on the otherwise darkened stage. To others, it is a beckoning light for all the mostly benevolent ghosts that are believed to occupy our stages at night. And to others, it is a symbol that the show must go on.

To me, the light that shines in the darkened theatre is
the imagination of the playwrights, creating their own
world of ideas, singing their songs of our humanity.
Quarantined, playwrights must continue to write, to be
that shining bulb. The chaos and death that surround us
as this virus ravages the world will most probably be
defeated within a year by our ingenuity. It is in the
penning of our playwrights that the triumph of the soul
will be nurtured, and the show will truly go on.

Watch for the **New Voices Holiday Anthology 2020**,
the next in our series, available in October.

John Bolen, Editor
Vice President
Former Producing Artistic Director
New Voices Playwrights Theatre
April 2020

Adrift in Time

By

John Franceschini

Adrift in Time was first produced at Stage Door Repertory in June, 2017, directed by Vanessa Evans and starred Carlos, Castellanos, Dee Shandera and Vanessa Evans.

John Franceschini is a playwright living in Southern California. He has been published by *Applause Theatrebooks* and *New Voices Playwrights Theatre.* John's plays have been produced in theatres across the U.S. including: Simpson College, IA; The Theatre at Hollywood and Vine, MA; Starlite Players, FL; Vienna Theatre Company, VA; Paw Paw Village Players, MI; The Globe Theatre, TX; Spokane Radio Theatre, WA; West Coast Players, FL; Pend Orielle Playhouse Community Theatre, WA; Stage Door Productions, VA; Downers Grove North High School IL; Wasatch Theatre Company, UT; Wells College, NY; Holton-Arms High School, MD, Madison Central High School, KY; Carroll College, MT;Bradley Playhouse, Conn; Stage Left Theatre, WA. In California at: Paper Wing Theatre; SkyPilot Theatre; Lonny Chapman Theatre; Found Theatre; Ohlone College; Three Roses Players; Theatre Out; Stage Door Repertory Theatre; Cabrillo Playhouse; Stages Theatre; Mysterium Theatre; and Empire Theatre. John is a member of: Dramatist Guild of America, New Voices Playwrights Theatre and Orange County Playwrights Alliance.

CHARACTERS

Malcolm, male, 20s, he is cynical about government, paranoid, perennially unemployed, with no ambition or prospects

Mom, female, 40s, a bit quirky, she wants her son Malcolm to get a job, get married and give her a grandchild

Starlight, female 20s, a free spirit who believes she is a time-traveler

> *It is present day in a row home in an east coast city. The setting is a working class living room. On a table are a handbag, a newspaper opened to a crossword puzzle, and envelopes. At rise, Malcolm is seated, working on a crossword puzzle. Mom enters.*

Mom: Malcolm! Are you still here!? I thought you were going to the job fair at the civic center.

Malcolm: 'Intellectually, stimulating experience.'

Mom: What?

Malcolm: The answer is eight letters.

Mom: Oh, for goodness sake! Take your head out of the crossword puzzle and listen to me.

Malcolm: I was thinking, 'math game', but that doesn't fit with the other clues.

Mom: I'm going to scream!

Malcolm: Nope, scream is six letters, doesn't count. Come on, Mom, try again.

Mom: Try 'head trip' because that's what you are.

Malcolm: Yeah, yeah! That fits perfectly. I knew you'd come through, Mom, you always do.

Mom: Why the hell are you still scribbling in the newspaper when you should be out searching for a paying job!?

Malcolm: It looked like it was going to rain. I didn't want to risk getting a cold, which, in my case, develops into congestion, a sore throat and fever.

Mom: The sun's shining, not a rain cloud in the sky.

Malcolm points out the window.

Malcolm: Just look out the window, Mom, I can see a cloud.

Mom: That's steam coming from the chimney at the shoe factory.

Malcolm: It's a rogue cloud just lingering, waiting for me to make a move outdoors. Then it'll pour while I'm waiting for the bus.

Mom: Good, then grab an umbrella and stand next to my car! It needs to be washed.

Malcolm: Very witty, Mother.

Mom: I heard the local library has an opening for a stacker. It's simple work; you put the returned books back in their proper place on a shelf.

Malcolm: Who holds a book anymore? That's so retro; everyone uses an I-Pad.

Mom: The job will be much easier then; fewer books to stack. Talk about an easy gig.

Malcolm: I'm not handling books with billions of germs on them.

Mom: Here we go again; you can wear gloves.

Malcolm: No dice; I refuse to be a government drone spying on people's reading habits. I'd be complicit in furthering the efforts off a totalitarian state. Big Brother is not getting his hooks into me. Screw Them!

Mom: What the hell are you talking about!? It's the county library. *(Beat.)* Besides, you might meet someone and make a friend. You could use one.

Malcolm: I have plenty of people to hang out with.

Mom mimes looking out a window.

Mom: Oh, I must be losing my eyesight, because I don't see the crowd waiting to come into the house.

Malcolm: Did you know more people are killed going to work than at any other time of day?

Mom: I just knew you would dodge the job fair today, so I scheduled an employment interview for you.

Malcolm: Whoa, whoa, what's this all about? *(Beat.)* My back's been acting up; traveling right now is out of the question.

Mom: It's a telephone interview, no travel involved... Wal-Mart is adding people in customer service for the Christmas season.

Malcolm: Will I have to speak with anyone? How close to me are customers going to stand? Do I have to touch them?

Mom: Did you not hear me; it's in customer service! What do you think? *(Beat.)* A man named Mr. Webster will contact you. I know him from church; he's doing me a favor. When he calls, put your best foot forward. *(Beat.)* Oh, by the way, I'm renting out your room at the end of the month.

Malcolm: What did you say!?

Mom: About Mr. Webster?

Malcolm: No, the other thing.

Mom: Ah, the room: I need the money. Since you're not bringing anything in, I have to find some other source.

Malcolm: You never mentioned any of this. We're a family unit, just you and me. I can't share space with anyone else.

Mom: When your father 'kicked the bucket' I got support money from Big Brother to help raise you. Which, by the way, you didn't complain about, as long as Uncle Sam was putting ham and eggs on the table.

Malcolm: Can't you get an extension from "The Man"?

Mom: That dried up years ago when you turned eighteen. I've been covering for your lazy ass since then. Ain't happening anymore; my full-time job turned into a part-time one. Unless you have a better idea, this is the next best thing.

Malcolm: Mom, don't do this to me. I'm your flesh and blood; we're bonded at the hip. You still have my shriveled umbilical cord on your bed stand.

Mom: Get it into your head; the Gravy Train has been derailed. Think of this as getting electric shock therapy, or a modified form of water-boarding; you'll come out of it a better man.

Malcolm: It'll be crowded with someone else living here. You won't have any privacy. Did you consider that?

Mom: Malcolm, you can always get your own place. Oh wait, that's right, you never established any credit. Or any money for a deposit. Because your life expectancy at any job you ever had was three days!

Malcolm: Come on, Mom, stop joking; we only have two bedrooms. There's no way any tenant is going to sleep on the sofa.

Mom: If I flip a coin, I wonder who will get the sofa.

Malcolm: I'm not giving up my bed to an outsider.

Mom: It won't be an outsider, it's Jessica: she runs the youth group at the church. She's coming over later to check out the set-up.

Malcolm: A woman is going to live with us!? I'll have to shave, stay dressed, and comb my hair...

Mom: I'm only following the advice of Dear Abby.

Malcolm: Who?

Mom: She writes an advice column in the newspaper. I wrote to her and she said I was making it too easy for you and should kick your ass out of the house. This would motivate you to jump start your life.

Malcolm: You put this out there for the whole world to see! Oh my God, I'll become the laughingstock of the neighborhood!

Mom: Relax, I didn't mention names. I just said, "My Son is a bum. What should I do?"

Malcolm: Gee thanks, Mom.

Mom: Make something of yourself; learn a skill. How on earth can you afford to get married? I'll never have grandkids. Do you ever think of "Dear Old Mom"? *(Beat.)* Wait, you're not gay, are you?

Malcolm: No, Mom, I date girls.

Mom: I mean it's okay if you are. Do you have a partner or whatever they call them? You know today, everything is on the table; no need to hide it. Bring him over sometime. Does he have a profession which pays good money?

Malcolm: Heterosexual, Mom. I'm heterosexual.

Mom: Is that why you never go anywhere? It's nothing to be ashamed about. *(Beat.)* If it were biblical days, you might get stoned to death, but today, everybody is out.

Malcolm: For the hundredth time, I'm straight. What do you want me to do? Knock up some girl?

Mom: That's not a bad idea. Then I'd have a grandchild.

Malcolm: I have a thought which will raise some serious money, so no need to rent out my room.

Mom: This is going to be a good one. Let's hear it.

Malcolm: I'll enter the "American Crossword Puzzle Tournament". It's in Vermont this year. First prize is seven thousand balloons. What'ya think? You only have to front me the two hundred dollar entry fee, airfare and hotel expenses.

Mom: Stop this pie-in-the-sky delusion. You can't get the simple clues in today's paper.

Malcolm: I'll have time to practice up. Are we a 'go' on this one, or what?

Mom: When Jessica gets here, be nice to her and don't swear. I think she was a nun once and lived in a convent. And tell her to wait for me; I have to run a quick errand.

> *Mom grabs a handbag and exits. Malcolm goes back to his crossword puzzle. A cell phone starts ringing. Malcolm answers it.*

Malcolm: Hello... Yes, this is Malcolm... Oh, Mr. Webster... Yes, Mom said you would call about a job in customer service... Before I answer your questions, do you mind if I ask you some quick ones? Here goes; am I allowed to smoke at the counter?... Oh, I see. Next question; what day of the week are drug tests given?... I need to know so I can call in sick that day... Okay, last question; Can I expect a promotion in two weeks?... Hello, hello, are you there?

> *Malcolm turns the cell phone off and does a fist pump.*

(To Himself.) Okay, one down and one to go. Now I need a plan to discourage Jessica from coming here. *(Beat.)* I think I'll trash my room; that should turn her off.

> *Malcolm quickly exits. Starlight suddenly comes bounding in and bounces and twirls to a stop. She seems momentarily disoriented.*

Starlight: Holy crap! When are they going to fix that time-travel machine!? Honestly, I'll rip them a new one when I get back.

> *Starlight taps her ear, as if there is a communicator in it.*

Hello, control center; are you there? Can you hear me? All I'm getting is static. I'm confirming the time-machine dropped me off in nineteen-seventy-seven.

> *Starlight looks around.*

Hey! Is anybody here? Hello! Hello!

> *Malcolm quickly enters.*

Malcolm: Who are you? How did you get in?

> *Starlight looks around.*

Starlight: Where's my luggage!? I had two bags when I entered the time-stream. Do you have them?

Malcolm: Oh, no you don't; Mom said you were just going to check out the room, not move in. Besides, it isn't ready for inspection.

Starlight: You'll have to help me look for them. You check all the rooms in the house; I'll take outside.

Malcolm: I'll do no such thing.

Starlight: Is this three-ten Elm Street?

Malcolm: Are you Jessica?

> *Starlight picks up pieces of mail from the table and checks the address.*

Starlight: This is the correct address; at least the control center got that right. *(Beat.)* Are you Professor Morton?

Malcolm: My name is Malcolm. You must know it; Mom would have told you.

Starlight: Where's Professor Morton?

Malcolm: There's no one here by that name.

Starlight: There has to be; our records are never wrong.

Malcolm: Is this some kind of gag? You're pulling my leg, right?

Starlight: Doesn't Charles Morton live at this address? He's a professor of physics at State University.

Malcolm: Oh, the Morton's; they moved out years ago. My grandparents bought the house from them.

Starlight: That can't be; I know I'm in the right location; this is the Morton residence. I need to talk with him. It's very important.

Malcolm: Well, if he were here, I guess you could. But since he's not, you have to leave. Adios, whoever you are.

Starlight: Find him for me. Use your computer and track him down.

Malcolm: Why should I? This is a two-way street. If you want my help, tell me your name and what you're up to.

Starlight: First, Google him just to confirm his location. I promise to tell you.

Malcolm: Do you keep your promises?

Starlight: Most days, but there are exceptions, like when you swear to love your lover but then a new flavor of the month comes by. It's out of my control; hormones get released, and then before you know it, it's Bing-Bang-Boom.

> *Malcolm pulls out his cell phone and works the keys.*

Malcolm: I don't know why I'm doing this, but if it helps get rid of you, I'll Google him... Here we go, I've found him.

Starlight: Great, I need to talk to him. Give me your phone!

Malcolm: That might be difficult to do unless you can conduct a séance. He passed away ten years ago.

Starlight: Impossible. He's forty-seven and in good health. *(Beat.)* Hold on; when did your grandparents buy this house?

Malcolm: Over forty years ago.

Starlight: Oh no, isn't this nineteen-seventy-seven?

> *Starlight goes to the table and picks up a newspaper.*

Malcolm: Are you going to tell me who you are? You promised!

Starlight: Oh shit, these monkey-brained dickheads missed by four decades. They pushed me out of the time-stream too soon. I was supposed to arrive in nineteen-seventy-seven.

Malcolm: What on earth are you talking about?

Starlight: I'm totally screwed. Now I'll never get my suitcases. *(Beat.)* Wait, unless they arrived forty years ago and were placed in the attic. *(Beat.)* Hey you, go up to the attic and look for two green bags.

Malcolm: Screw you! Now, get out of the house! Otherwise, you'll be doing time in the pokey.

Starlight: Do you know how to use a slide rule?

Malcolm: What's a slide rule?

Starlight: Terrific, just my luck. I get a dummy.

Malcolm: Well, are you going to tell me?

Starlight: It's used in trigonometry; Professor Morton knew how to use one. Now I have to find someone else.

Malcolm: Come on, are you really Jessica? Did Mom send you here?

Starlight faces downstage.

Starlight: Other time-travelers got juicier assignments like, "Bring back Albert Einstein or Thomas Edison." What task do they give me; bring back some schlub who knows how to use a slide rule.

Malcolm: Listen, Jessica, you're not making a lot of sense. But, if you're heading up the youth group, maybe you can get some 'weed'?

Starlight: What to do?... What to do?

Malcolm: Did Mom give you a key? Is that how you got inside?

Starlight: The time-stream dropped me off.

Malcolm: Is that a new transportation service, like Uber?

Starlight: Think of it as a subway line traveling through time. You hop on, tell them where and when to deliver you and they push you out at the precise moment. Only in this case, the jackass did it too early. I wasn't supposed to exit now, but further back in time. I'm a time-traveler.

Malcolm: This is so sci-fi; what a fabulous story. Are you a writer?

Starlight: Since I'll be here for a while, you should know my name is Starlight. I've already told you too much.

Malcolm: Is that the name you use when writing?

Starlight extends one arm and walks around the room.

Starlight: That's the name issued to me by the state.

Malcolm: Why are you doing that?

Starlight: Trying to locate the time-stream. If it's still here, I can jump back in.

Malcolm: As much as I'd like to believe you, time travel isn't possible.

Starlight: In the twenty-fourth century, earth is hit with a giant solar flare which fries all electronics. Everything has to be rebuilt but people are so dependent on technology, their brains have turned to Jell-O.

Malcolm: What a super plotline, But there's a flaw; all they have to do is look up the solutions in a book.

> *Starlight continues to walk around with her arm extended.*

Starlight: No physical books exist; all the knowledge is stored in the 'cloud' and downloaded to a nano-chip in one's brain. And guess what? The 'cloud' connection was toasted. So... here we are.

Malcolm: What a dilemma; you're building suspense with the story. Tell me more. What happens next?

Starlight: The government sent time-travelers to find people with specific skills and bring them into the future to fix what we need.

> *Starlight takes a few steps and jumps forward. She looks around.*

Crap! I missed it; I'm still here.

Malcolm: Hey, if you are really from the future, tell me who's going to win the Super Bowl game this year. I can make a future in Vegas. I'll never have to look for a job again.

Starlight: Sports were never my thing.

> *Malcolm is rubbing his hands.*

Malcolm: Okay, how about a hot stock, you know; something that will go right through the roof?

Starlight: It could alter the future. We're not supposed to tamper with anything.

Malcolm: Oh, come on. Just one technology company like the next Facebook or Apple; I won't tell anyone.

Starlight: Maybe we can buy a slide rule and an instruction book?

Malcolm: What about people you take into the future. Don't they learn all the secrets?

Starlight: Their memory about what happened to them is erased. And then they're returned to their own time. *(Beat.)* Do you have a mother? Do you live together?

Malcolm: Of course. Why would you say that?

Starlight: The state controls everything. They take all your eggs, fertilize one and grow the fetus in an incubator tank. No one knows their biological mother. You grow up without parents. *(Beat.)* I heard that a woman can feel a baby kick in her uterus. I'd like to experience that someday.

> *Starlight jumps forward again.*

The time-stream is not here; probably because it is waiting in this house, but back in nineteen-seventy-seven. *(Beat.)* Hey, wait a minute; that gives me an idea.

Malcolm: I'd like to live in the future to see what it's like.

Starlight: Too many people, not enough food; if you get hungry, the state sends a message to a chip in your brain. It compresses your stomach and you think you've had a meal.

Malcolm: That won't work for me. I like to have a Big-Mac and fries now and then.

Starlight: There's no religion; you can only believe in the state.

Malcolm: I kinda don't go to church right now anyway. But Mom would be bummed out by that,

Starlight: You're only allowed to have one friend, which has to be approved by the state.

Malcolm: Wow! Talk about Big Brother; you're not painting a fun place to live in. This story is bumming me out.

Starlight: It's the truth, Malcolm. I am from the future and I've just made a decision... I'm not going back. I'll stay with you Malcolm.

Malcolm: You and Me! Will you really!? No, you're pulling my leg; this is a gag. Mom cooked this up, didn't she?

Starlight: You know the state will look for me, but never find me. They'll search in nineteen-seventy-seven where I should be; but not now. So, I'm perfectly safe.

Malcolm: So, you really are from the future.

> *Mom enters, without looking up. She places her handbag on the table.*

Mom: Malcolm, Jessica can't make it tonight. *(To Starlight.)* Oh, Hello. Are you one of Malcolm's friends?

Starlight: My name is Starlight. I'm a time-traveler from the future, the twenty-fourth century. I came here in the time-stream.

Mom: Of course, you are. *(Beat.)* Are you a flight attendant on this time machine?

Starlight: Heavens no, I'm just a passenger. Others push you out when your time-window appears.

Mom: How long are you going to stay, Starlight?

Starlight: Oh, probably forever.

Mom: Do you have a job?

Malcolm: How could she, Mom!? She's not from here.

Mom: *(Sarcastically.)* How foolish of me to think that; another mouth to feed. Why not?

Starlight: I'm a friend of Malcolm's; we plan to get engaged.

Malcolm: *(Excitedly.)* WE DO! OH BOY!

> *Malcolm quickly starts rubbing his hands together. Mom looks upward and raises her arms.*

Mom: Praise the Lord! A real live girl! *(To Malcolm.)* Malcolm, now you can throw away that blow-up doll you have in your room.

Starlight: Oh, yes; Malcolm's going to give me a baby.

Malcolm: Hey, this is starting to sound better all the time! *(Beat.)* Starlight, can we start right away?

Mom: Finally, I'll get to be a grandmother!

Starlight: We're going to name the baby Moonbeam.

Mom: What a lovely name. *(Beat.)* Now, Malcolm, you'll have to find a job to support your wife and baby, won't you?

Malcolm: Yeah, Mom; I'll call Mr. Webster back at Wal-Mart. We got disconnected before.

> *Mom answers her cell phone and moves downstage. Malcolm and Starlight move stage right and mime talking.*

Mom: Hello, Ethyl... No, I didn't hear any news, I just got home... Really! The police are looking for an escaped patient from the sanatorium... Spotted in our neighborhood. Are you certain?... Is she dangerous?... Well, that's good... What?... She claims to be from the future, you say?... What does she look like...

> *Mom looks Starlight up and down.*

Yes, my doors are locked. If I see anyone like that, I'll contact the police. Bye.

Malcolm: Who was that, Mom?

Mom: Ethyl. She just wanted to ask about a recipe. *(Beat.)* So, Starlight, why don't you stay for dinner?

Starlight: That would be wonderful.

Mom: In fact, we have an empty bedroom. You could move in now if you like. Stay as long as you want. Isn't that right, Malcolm?

Malcolm: Yeah, great idea, Mom!

Starlight: Can I call you Mom?

Mom: Why not? Join the club. *(Beat.)* I have an idea. Why don't we change the color of your hair tonight?

> *The lights quickly fade.*

<u>End of play.</u>

Backs

By

Lynne Bolen

Lynne Bolen is a playwright, director, producer, and actor. Her play, *Assumptions*, is included in Best American Short Plays 2011-2012, *Boulevard of Broken Dreams* in Best American Short Plays 2013-2014, and *Baggage Game* in Best 5-Minute Plays, all published by Applause Theatre & Cinema Books. Her plays published in the New Voices Annual Anthology include *Spanish Masters* (2014), *Winners* (2015), *True Confessions* (2016), *A Fair to Remember* (2017), *Samantha Heart, P.I.* (2018), *Chicken Game* (2019); and in the New Voices Holiday Plays, *Christmastime Machine* (2017) *Past, Future & Christmas Present* (2018), and *On Target* [musical] (2019). Lynne's plays have been produced at Lion's Paw Theatre, St. Louis, MO; Niagara Univ, NY; Acadia Univ, Nova Scotia; Univ of Maryland; Univ of Rhode Island; Arizona State Univ; Univ of Northwestern, MN; Bethel College, KS; DePaul College Prep, IL; Hotchkiss School, CT; Oak Park High, CA; Drama West Productions; Stage Door Repertory Theatre; MUZEO; OC Pavilion Performing Arts Center; Chance Theater; Vanguard Theatre; Gallery Theatre; STAGEStheatre; Cabrillo Playhouse; Empire Theatre; Mysterium Theater. Lynne has directed and produced dozens of shows. As an actor, Lynne has appeared in many stage productions, award winning films, and music videos.

<u>CHARACTERS</u>

Kimberly, female, 20s-30s

Kaitlin, female, 20s-30s

Kristina, female 20s-30s

> *The setting is Friday, 9:00pm in June at a cocktail party at Kimberly's condo. Kimberly's kitchen has a table at center stage. Platters and bowls are scattered on the table along with a glass of wine. An ice chest is on the floor. The living room is off-stage, and the patio is off-stage on the other side. At rise, Kimberly, wearing fancy cocktail party attire, is opening a bag of Salt and Black Pepper Kettle Chips. Kaitlin, wearing business attire, enters from the living room, carrying her cell phone and an ice bucket.*

Kimberly*:* Hey, Kaitlin! I was beginning to worry whether you were going to show up.

Kaitlin: *(Setting ice bucket and cell phone on the table.)* I got here in time for an empty ice bucket, wouldn't you know it.

Kimberly: Would you mind refilling it? There are bags of ice in the cooler.

Kaitlin: Sure, no problem; the faster I can get a drink. Happy <u>Un</u>birthday, Kimberly! You look beautiful!

> *Kaitlin and Kimberly hug.*

Kimberly: Thank you, I'm so happy that my friends are here for my special day.

Kaitlin fills the ice bucket.

Kaitlin: I'm so happy we're friends. Do people even get the "unbirthday"?

Kimberly pours chips into the bowl.

Kimberly: Some have asked, so I've told them I celebrate my half-birthday in June because I was born on Christmas. Others just think it's a fun reason to throw a cocktail party, which it is.

Kaitlin: Everyone loves a party.

Kimberly: You know, I spent a lot of time putting together some fabulous hors d'oeuvres, but the only thing they all seem to be eating is chips!

Kaitlin: Well, Salt and Black Pepper Kettle Chips are the best! I'm starving. What kind of fabulous hors d'oeuvres did you make?

Kimberly: Eggplant caviar, zucchini crisps, tomato tartlets, dill cucumber toasties, roasted chickpeas, kale chips...

Kaitlin: Really, Kimberly, all vegan at a cocktail party?

Kimberly: Justin brought some meatballs.

Kaitlin: Justin from Marketing? *(Kimberly smiles and nods.)* Justin brought meatballs? Wow! I didn't take time to change. I just came straight from work.

Kimberly: It's almost 9:00 on Friday night! Why were you still at work?

Kaitlin: *(Miffed.)* I had to finish an analysis for Kristina tonight.

Kimberly: Tonight? She really didn't ask for it tonight, did she? It's my unbirthday party.

Kaitlin: *(Angrily.)* Kristina said she needed the analysis by the end of the day. I e-mailed it at 8:00pm so technically, I beat the end of day by four hours. I'm so mad at her! She knew I was looking forward to your party. She'd better be working hard on her report tonight!

Kimberly: Kaitlin, you must have misunderstood her. I don't think she wanted you to stay at the office and come to the party late.

Kaitlin: *(Shouting.)* You don't think? You don't know. Kristina can be infuriatingly manipulative. She wanted the analysis tonight, so I worked my butt off until 8:00pm to finish it. Why are you defending her? Unbelievable. I need a drink!

 Kaitlin storms off to the living room.

Kimberly: *(Calling after her.)* Kaitlin! 0 to 100 real fast!

 *Kristina, wearing a glittery dress and high
 heels, and carrying a cocktail, enters from the
 patio.*

Kristina: It's a little chilly outside. What are you doing in the kitchen?

Kimberly: It's a little chilly inside. (*Beat.*) I'm just refilling potato chips, and getting yelled at.

Kristina: Who would yell at you on your unbirthday?

Kimberly: Kaitlin.

Kristina: Kaitlin? Great, she's finally here! I wonder why she's so late.

Kimberly: It's your fault, Kristina.

Kristina: My fault, what? Why was she yelling at you?

Kimberly: You made her stay at work until 8:00.

Kristina: No way!

Kimberly: That's what she said.

Kristina: That's ridiculous.

Kimberly: She said you asked her to do an analysis by EOD. She finished at 8:00.

Kristina: I didn't say I needed it tonight. Your party is tonight.

Kimberly: You didn't ask her to send the analysis by **End of Day**?

Kristina: No, I said it would be great to have it by **COB**, *but only if possible.* I absolutely did not ask her to stay late to finish.

Kimberly: I think Kaitlin interpreted **Close of Business** as **End of Day**.

Kristina: They are two different times. **COB** means 5:00pm, and **EOD** means by midnight. Kaitlin knows the difference.

Kimberly: Apparently she doesn't, or she wouldn't be furious with you.

Kristina: Furious with me? I thought she was yelling at you!

Kimberly: Yes, she was!

Kristina: Why?

Kimberly: Because I had your back, Kristina. She was mad that I was defending you.

Kristina: Thanks, but why would you need to defend me?

Kimberly: I said I didn't think you would have told her the analysis was needed **EOD** when you knew my party was tonight. I said that I thought she misunderstood you.

Kristina: (*Agitated.*) You're so right. Now I'm mad. She's blaming me for working late? Did she actually say I said **EOD**? Because I positively said **COB**.

Kimberly: I don't know. Settle down.

Kristina: You need to remember whether Kaitlin said **EOD**, because if so, she is lying. I specifically said **COB** not **EOD**. Think, Kimberly!

Kimberly: (*Heatedly.*) Now <u>you</u> are yelling at me! You girls need to chill. I'm done.

Kimberly takes the bowl of chips to the patio.

Kristina: *(Calling after her.)* Off to the vape zone again?

> *Kaitlin, highball in hand, enters from the living room.*

Kaitlin: I left my cell phone. Oh, I thought Kimberly was here.

Kristina: She went out to the patio... again.

Kaitlin: *(Coldly.)* Look at you, all glammed gorgeous, and me all business boring. Aren't you supposed to be working on your report tonight?

Kristina: No, you are well aware that Kimberly's unbirthday party has been on the calendar for weeks.

Kaitlin: And yet, you asked me to finish my analysis by the end of the day, which I did, leaving me no time to get dressed up, like you.

Kristina: Kimberly told me that you misunderstood my request.

Kaitlin: Misunderstood? That's what she said to me, too. I did not misunderstand, Kristina. You wanted the analysis by the end of the day.

Kristina: I did not say I needed it tonight. The party is tonight. I said it would be great to have it by **COB**, *but only if possible*. I did not ask you to stay late to finish.

Kaitlin: **COB**, **EOD**, they're the same.

Kristina: They are two different times. **COB** means 5:00pm, and **EOD** means by midnight. I thought you knew the difference.

Kaitlin: Apparently not, or I wouldn't be furious with you.

Kristina: Kaitlin, it was just a miscommunication. I asked for the analysis this morning, and didn't think it would take you that long. I'm really sorry. I don't plan to continue working on my report until Monday **BOD**. *(She smiles.)* **Beginning of Day**. Hey, in the future, I will be sure to specify the actual time that I need something, not a **TLA**.

Kaitlin: What's a **TLA**?

Kristina: *(Smiles.)* Three letter acronym. *(Beat.)* So, apologies. Are we okay?

Kaitlin: Well, the analysis really didn't take that long. I wasn't able to start it until late afternoon. *(Beat.)* I suppose it's actually good to have the work finished now so I don't have to worry about it over the weekend. I guess we're okay.

Kristina: Good. I'm sorry you didn't get to the party until late. You must have been famished. Did you get something to eat?

Kaitlin: I just wish I had changed my clothes. I had some kale chips.

Kristina: They're pretty tasty, right?

Kaitlin: *(Dissing.)* I cannot believe the appetizers that Kimberly made. All vegan! What was she thinking? A party is not a party without wings, ribs, Lit'l Smokies, and a cheese platter.

Kristina: You should give her hors d'oeuvres a try. They are delicious and very nicely presented. Kimberly did a lovely job.

Kaitlin: You sure have her back!

Kristina: I don't know why. Justin did bring meatballs, but they are long gone.

Kaitlin: I'm surprised she invited Justin.

Kristina: She has been out there with him all night. It's sickening. She just went outside again.

Kaitlin: What are you saying? Is Kimberly flirting with Justin?

Kristina: Yeah, and I am pissed. She knows that you have a thing for him. I was planning to leave when I ran into her before you came in.

Kaitlin: Why are you leaving?

Kristina: Because I have your back, too! I wasn't going to stay at her party and watch her hit on him while you were not here.

Kaitlin: Wow, thanks, Kristina, but it's not fair for you to leave the party on my account.

Kristina: I've had enough to drink and you're hungry. Want to go to In-N-Out?

Kaitlin: Yeah, there's nothing good to eat here, but I only just arrived. People will wonder if we leave before the cake.

Kristina: Nobody would care. Who throws a party for herself? So weird; unbirthday.

Kaitlin: You know, ever since Kimberly was a kid, her parents threw her unbirthday parties so she could have a special celebration day of her own She told me they would always sing "A Very Merry Unbirthday" at her parties, from <u>Alice in Wonderland</u>.

Kristina: Now she's using it as an excuse for a meatless cocktail party. Omigod, do you think the cake will be vegan?

Kaitlin: I understand why you want to leave, Kristina, but we really should stay. For Kimberly.

> *Kimberly overhears while entering from the patio.*

Kimberly: So you want to leave?

Kaitlin: No, we're not leaving. We're having an awesome time.

Kristina: Speak for yourself.

Kimberly: Kaitlin, thanks for having my back.

Kaitlin: Hey, Kimberly, I shouldn't have yelled at you. I was mad at Kristina and felt you were taking her side against me. I'm sorry.

Kimberly: No worries. Looks like the two of you are all good now.

Kaitlin: Just a miscommunication.

Kimberly: *(Coldly.)* Well, it sounds like everything is just fine, then.

Kristina: *(Sarcastically.)* Right.

Kimberly: Kristina, I really did not appreciate your yelling at me about COB and EOD. What is your problem?

Kristina: My problem? OMG. You're the problem!

Kimberly: What the hell have I done to you? I had your back with Kaitlin.

Kristina: And now you're stabbing her in the back.

Kimberly: Are you crazy? What have I done to Kaitlin?

Kristina: You know she likes Justin, but you've been flirting with him all night.

Kimberly: You are crazy! I'm not stabbing Kaitlin in the back. I <u>have</u> her back! I barely know Justin, but I went up to Marketing and invited him for Kaitlin. I didn't think he was going to come, because he said he already made plans with a college buddy who moved into town. I told him to bring his friend along.

Kristina: The tall guy?

Kimberly: The fun, incredibly good-looking, tall guy. I have been outside trying to cozy up with Jason the hunk, not Justin from Marketing.

Kaitlin: You invited Justin for me?

Kimberly: Yes, sweetie, I have your back. I'm not stabbing it, like someone is accusing me of doing.

Kristina: It really looked to me like... I guess I misunderstood. Seems I'm having to say I'm sorry a lot tonight. Sorry.

Kaitlin: Just a miscommunication.

Kimberly: No harm, no foul.

Kristina: Cool. Happy unbirthday, Kimberly!

Kaitlin: A very merry unbirthday, to you!

Kimberly: The three of us are such good friends. We're the Three Amigos. The Three Stooges. The Three Musketeers.

Kristina: Kimberly, Kaitlin, Kristina. The three K's.

Kaitlin: KKK; um, not good.

Kimberly: We're the Backs!

Kristina: What, like football? Quarterbacks? Halfbacks? Fullbacks?

Kimberly: *(Patting their backs.)* No, like we have each others' backs.

Kaitlin: All for one and one for all.

Kimberly: *(Raising her glass.)* To us, to friendship, to...

>*All three toast.*

All: ...the Backs!

End of play.

Barely Beige

By

David Rusiecki

David Rusiecki is the president of the New Voices Playwrights Theatre. A member since 2009, he has contributed to New Voices Playwrights Theatre as a writer, director, actor and co-producer. He has also served as head of the New Works Festival Literary Committee and Board of Trustees with the Long Beach Playhouse. His full-length **Sides** was selected for the Long Beach Playhouse New Works table-read series while in the same year **...Prep...** received honorable mention with Panndora Productions' annual festival of new play readings. His one-act play **Kid Gloves** (originally entitled **Have A Nice Day**) has been published in *The Best American Short Plays 2012-2013* (Applause Books) as well as in *Best Monologues from Best American Short Plays* (Applause Books). His one-act play **Long Time Coming** has been published in *The Best American Short Plays 2014-2015* (Applause Books). Other. one-act plays produced by New Voices Playwrights Theatre include **Mistle-in-Tow** at Stages Theatre (Fullerton, CA) along with **Two-Some, A Fake Christmas, The Big 3-0, $ecret $anta, Long Time Coming, Holiday Hoo-Ha, Return To Sender, Have A Nice Day**, and **Last Call** at Stage Door Repertory Theatre (Anaheim, CA). Other full-length works which received staged readings include **Groupie** at Theatre Out (Santa Ana, CA) as well as **Scattered Showers, The Wrecking Ball** and **Goon** at Stage Door Repertory Theatre. He can be reached at: djrusiecki@gmail.com

CHARACTERS

Zara – female, mid 20s, Indian

Guy – male, 20s

Date – male, 20s

Father & daughter & Mover – non-speaking

Scene 1

> *Lights rise on a dark studio apartment. The only light we see is the digital clock from Zara's nightstand next to her bed. Suddenly, we hear the sound of the door opening. Zara and a guy, mid 20s, stumble in while kissing. She has a purse and notepad in her hand. She leads him inside and shuts the door behind them. They begin kissing again until she stops. She flicks on a nearby floor lamp.*

Zara: Oh boy…

Guy: What?

Zara: Nothing. That was fun. You're a fun kisser.

> *They kiss again until she stops. Zara attempts to walk past but he blocks her path.*

What are you doing?

Guy: You mean, that's it? No more?

> *She attempts to walk past him again but he steps in front to block her.*

Zara: You're clever.

Guy: I'm horny.

Zara: What a lovely sentiment.

Guy: Aren't you?

Zara: I was, a few minutes ago… before you revealed your true colors.

Guy: You play your cards right, I'll give you something really revealing.

> *She reaches for the doorknob, and opens the door.*

Zara: Um, I'm going to leave this door open. That way my neighbors don't think I'm stealing their Washington Post.

Guy: Come on, what is this?

Zara: The end of our pleasant evening.

Guy: You can't be serious?

Zara: Afraid so, Johnny Mac.

Guy: I don't believe this.

> *She manages to walk past him. She tosses her notepad on the coffee table. She opens up her hand purse and rummages through.*

Guy: What is it with you? Is this like, something you do to every fucking guy you meet?

Zara: Most of them, yes.

Guy: You're... Jesus, I don't know… crazy.

Zara: I try.

She pulls out some cash and hands it to him.

Guy: What's this?

Zara: Cab fare.

Guy: You're sending me home?

Zara: I'm tired and don't feel like arguing.

Guy: But I thought that… you wanted me to stay over.

Zara: You're sadly mistaken.

Guy: So, this is it? We're not going to do anything?

Zara: It's late, the Metro buses stopped running.

Guy: But, five bucks?

Zara: Oh, okay.

She opens her purse and gives him another dollar.

Here, six should cover it.

Guy: Seriously?

Zara: This is for walking me back to my place in one piece.

She walks over to him and gently nudges him out of her apartment.

Guy: Wait, can I call you? Maybe… you know, we could meet up some time.

Zara: Absolutely, I'll look you up. Bye…

She shuts the door in his face.

(To audience.) Well… that was eventful.

> *She locks the door, looks through the peephole then turns around and sighs, lifting her head up to the ceiling. She leans against the door.*

Most boys just take their cue and depart with their pride fully intact. I wouldn't lose too much sleep over him. This time next week he'll be back in his girlfriend's arms. Completely oblivious this encounter ever took place. What I neglected to tell him was I never allow anyone to stay over. My apartment is off limits for anybody from the outside. This is my sanctuary. It's weird, I know. I mean, how do you explain that to someone you meet in line at a local, late-night chili bowl establishment. Besides, I like scaring people.

> *She checks the peephole again.*

Finally, I think he got the picture. Didn't know how long it would take to sink in. That's it; I refuse to open the door again tonight. The store is officially closed for business.

> *She turns and makes her way inside her studio apartment. With each light she turns on we see a bathroom door, a loveseat against the wall, a laptop on a coffee table in front of the loveseat, a bookshelf console filled with nothing but books except for a record player in the center, stereo speakers on the floor next to milk crates with magazines, records, a full-length mirror, a*

*beanbag in the middle of the room, a tiny walk-
in kitchen, a kitchen table with two chairs and
her queen size bed and night stand leaned up
against the other side of the wall.*

You're probably wondering, how did this poor girl end
up in this dreadful situation?

*She begins to remove her shoes, jacket and
other wardrobe items while changing into more
comfortable sleepwear.*

Tonight I made my way to this monthly woman's
spoken word event. Down the way from here. Very
well attended, about fifty patrons or so; which is how
many seats this venue can hold. Anyhow, I know the
person who runs this group and they keep pestering me
to get on stage. I put it off the past few months until
finally I acquiesced. It was a hybrid of poetry readings,
spoken word, standup, more poetry reading…
celebrating the empowerment of women, our
intersectional place in the workforce… all those fancy
buzzwords. Not that I'm ridiculing them or looking my
nose down upon what these people do. It's admirable
work, putting together a monthly event where women
writers, artists and performers get to be seen and heard.
I just… how do I say this politely, I don't enjoy their
company as much as I feel I should. I mean, they're so
serious about what they do… which is good, I suppose.
Lord knows I'm too lazy to pull off what they
accomplished tonight. But once all the pleasant chit-
chat subsides, I really don't have much in common with
them. Of course, I can't say all this, all of what I'm
telling you… I can't really say this to any of them.
They love me, I put up with them. And no, I didn't get
paid for my involvement, I didn't ask or expect any

financial compensation from them… and that's basically where we stand.

She lifts up her notepad and places it on her nightstand.

Like I mentioned before, they simply adore me. They don't worship me the way goddesses or idols are supposed to be worshipped. They don't even view me as the clumsy clot you see in front of you. But I get the impression I'm more like a... a symbol to them, some representation of a certain demographic… in this instance, Hindu. Desperately wanting to include me for their movement. And these are highly educated, highly privileged, highly professional women we're talking about here. But, come on… to schedule this event on a <u>Saturday</u> night? I mean, where's the logic in that?

She sighs and goes over to her record collection.

Think about it, what's the one thing missing from these monthly women's meetings? Oh yes… <u>men</u>! All these self-professed, pseudo-intellectuals standing around the reception area nibbling on their herb fresh goat cheese and multi grain crispbread, sipping on plastic cups of sulfate-filled Sauvignon Blanc from New Zealand… if they're so brilliant in their fields, how come there's no bloody men in attendance! I mean, seriously how do they expect me to meet any handsome, self-respecting squire at some makeshift art gallery on a Saturday night? Forget about them, I've got <u>my</u> own movement to worry about.

She pulls out a record from the crate.

Take for example, him.

> *She displays to the audience a 33-LP of "My Aim Is True" by Elvis Costello.*

The one, the only… Declan Patrick MacManus. That's his birth name. Most of you may know him by his stage name: Elvis Costello. Of course, the only Elvis you bloody Yanks seem to recognize is the one buried in Tennessee.

> *She gazes at the album cover.*

Absurdist, clown, joker, tragic hero, virtuoso, genius… no good words come to mind to perfectly define his musical legacy. More so than anything, I'm more drawn to his compelling sense of perception, lyrically. I'd play you something from this to give you an example but since I'm the DJ and it's way late in the evening, my bloody head's starting to wind down. I need something a little more… slower in tempo.

> *She puts it back in the crate and goes digging through her collection.*

For your information, music is my first true love. Before literature, before science, before art. aspects, I suppose it's a healthy obsession.

> *She pulls out a 33-LP of "East Side Story" by Squeeze.*

Here we go, perfect.

> *She pulls out the vinyl record and places it on the turntable. She carefully drops the needle on the record. We hear the song "Tempted."*

Bear with me for a sec.

> *She disappears into the bathroom. She returns*
> *holding a hand towel, wiping her face.*

The brilliance is this song benefits from Elvis
Costello's input. You see, he co-produced this album.
His fingerprints are all over these tracks. You can hear
him singing in the background… listen.

> *She stares off in the distance, then turns to the*
> *full-length mirror, picks up a hairbrush and*
> *mimes singing holding the hairbrush as a*
> *microphone.*

Timeless, absolutely brilliant. On first listen, it's simply
impossible to put your finger on the year this was
recorded. A charming melody about a two-timing,
backstabbing bastard. That's the wonderful duality of
music.

> *She continues staring at the mirror.*

'I said to my reflection, let's get out of this place…'

Scene 2

> *Lights rise on Zara in her studio apartment. She*
> *wears sweatpants and sweatshirt, folding*
> *clothes in a laundry basket. From her stereo, we*
> *hear 'Love Is a Losing Game" by Amy*
> *Winehouse.*

Zara: Sunday morning… my absolute favorite day, my
favorite time of the week.

> *In the kitchen area, we see a father slow*
> *dancing with his infant daughter standing on his*

shoes, holding his hands for balance. Zara doesn't notice.

My partiality to the last day of the week stems from growing up and trying on new outfits in my bedroom. With the intention of attending Sunday matinee performances with Tata, my father... that's my name for him... donning his usual suit and tie. Shoes polished. You see, once a month my dad would take me to a Sunday matinee show of my choice. While most of friends' families would get dressed and attend church services, I painted the town, so to speak, with Tata. Take your pick... musical, play, ballet, Shakespeare, the symphony, opera. No shortage of cultural fine arts in our Nation's Capital. We always started our Father-Daughter routine with brunch. Sometimes my favorite Tex-Mex restaurant on Wisconsin. Other days, dining at a coffee shop off Massachusetts Avenue. Or, my personal favorite, the Kennedy Center Rooftop Terrace.

The father finishes dancing with the girl. They exit.

As for my Mum, she passed five years ago. Brain aneurism. Long before that, she handed over her love of literature to me. And fine writing. And feminist writing.

She pulls out a book from the shelf.

Betty Friedan, <u>The Feminine Mystique</u>... you see, I'm not completely oblivious to the movement. The seeds were planted early in my formative years.

She puts the book back in the shelf.

I was never allowed to watch much television, unless it was British programming. As of this day I don't own a

TV. Takes up too much space, most shows put me to sleep.

She pulls out a framed picture.

While my Mum did take me to films, she never once got between me and my Dad on our outings. In fact, it was her suggestion. She knew the value of our 'alone time' together, me being an only child. Every time I'm on the bus and we ride past Sibley Hospital, I think of her.

She puts the frame back on the shelf.

Me, I was born in Malta, where my family lived for three years. I don't remember any of it. My father was a foreign minister. In charge of maintaining diplomatic and bilateral relations between the Maltese and Indians. He made many trips going back and forth from New Delhi and Mumbai. Again, not that I remember these things. Just going off what I was told to me. After I turned three, we relocated to England, where I maintain my dual citizenship. I still have my English passport somewhere in this clutter.

She turns her head looking around the room.

We lived outside London for a bit. Then by the time I was five, we moved here to DC. And since then I haven't lived anywhere else. My father on the other hand moved back to London, after Mum's passing. We no longer do our father-daughter outings on a regular basis, the thing I miss the most. But on a positive note, he'll be arriving shortly in New York where we've arranged to meet for dinner this Saturday and take in a show. He said he has something important to tell me in person. I have news for him too, I can't wait.

Barely Beige

Scene 3

Lights rise on Zara sitting at a coffee shop with her date across from her. She has on a soccer jersey. They both have coffee mugs in front of them. His back is to the audience.

Date: I see you're a Liverpool fan.

She turns to the audience.

Zara: See what I have to deal with?

She turns back to him.

Date: You have on LFC.

Zara: I just like the way football jerseys look on me.

Date: I'm a Chelsea fan myself. So, what is it you do?

Zara: You mean, as a profession?

Date: Yeah.

Zara: Um, a few things.

Date: Like?

Zara: I write a column.

Date: Who do you write for?

Zara: City Paper, I'm a critic.

Date: What do you critique?

Zara: Cultural critic… food, music, art.

Date: Interesting. What else do you like?

She turns to the audience.

Zara: Should I talk to him about books? How about poetry? Should I reveal that I attended a private, Catholic, all-girls academy not far from here? What will he think of when he finds out I also went to an all-girls Catholic university? You mention that to people, especially men, you see the "L" word start to form across their forehead. So do I casually divulge my sexual history? Which was really nothing to write about in the first place. Okay, I had some experiences with other women… but I never followed through with them. The closest I ever came to was my best friend growing up. Before she away for college, we had a final girls-night out together; just the two of us. We wound up in her bed together. But before we could say or do anything the next day, she up and moved out of town. Never to return again to the District. In the meantime, let's spice up this drab conversation a bit.

She turns back to him.

Zara: Sooo, are you a grower or a shower?

Date: Um, what?

Zara: I asked, are you a "grower?" Or a "shower"?

Date: I'm not sure I get what…

Zara: Your penis. I'm asking, are you comfortable in what you're packing? Thus, would you consider yourself a grower in the sense you gain more proportionally when you get aroused? Or do you find yourself just… well, I guess, naturally well-hung?

Date: Wow… nobody's ever asked me that before.

She smiles to audience.

<u>Scene 4</u>

Lights rise on Zara's apartment. She's wearing casual attire. She has her nightstand lamp and other table lamps switched on. She has an open suitcase on top of her bed, packing items in it.

Zara: In a few short hours I'm off for New York to see Tata. I'll stay overnight with him then be back here before I fly out to Iowa on Monday.

She studies her suitcase for a moment then goes to her bookshelf. She retrieves a wrapped book.

I get to share with him one of my published essays in this volume. This is his copy.

She goes back to the suitcase and carefully packs the book in her luggage.

As usual I don't expect him to be overly enthusiastic. Unless of course I follow it up with an engagement announcement. "No, Tata… I haven't found anyone… not yet." It's like the conversation finishes right there. I'm almost twenty-five with no marital prospect… according to him, I'm done. I've become a walking cliché. You hear people say, "it's the nonstop pressure." Or "the ostracizing women endure from their parents". The truth is, regardless of whatever professional feats I accomplish, whether I become a published author or a literary professor… you hear the same response: "… sorry, next contestant...". I mean, the expectations are ridiculous. Which I believe is why having the Atlantic Ocean between us makes our relationship somewhat manageable.

> *She attempts to zip up her bag. The zipper gets stuck. She reopens the bag and thrusts her hand inside maneuvering items around.*

I don't want to be pushed into something I don't want to do. At the sake of sounding overly maudlin, I sometimes find myself asking… what defines me? As a woman or as an individual? Better yet, why am I talking like this? Where's my bloody Saturday night women's group when I need them?

> *She finishes stuffing then begins to pound on the bag. She holds one hand down firmly on the bag and the other hand steering the zipper around. She successfully closes it.*

There, I'm ready… I think.

<u>Scene 5</u>

> *Lights rise on Zara's apartment. It is completely dark except for the digital clock on Zara's nightstand next to her bed. Everything is silent and still for a moment until we hear a phone ringing. The ringing stops for a moment then followed by a voice message:*

Male Voice: Sweetheart… darling… where are you?.. I'm terribly sorry about what happened… I, I don't know what else to tell you... I wish that you would… understand somehow… what was I supposed to, how was I to know you would react in such a fashion… I have no clue where to reach you... Honey, please… please return my call… I have to fly back to London tomorrow… I hate to part like this… please don't do this, don't respond this way… get back to me once you receive this… I'm still at the hotel… please, please let me know you're okay.

> *We hear the phone hang up followed by a dial tone.*

<u>Scene 6</u>

> *Lights rise on Zara's apartment. The early morning light peaks through the windows. Suddenly, we hear the sound of the door opening. Zara appears at the doorstep dragging her suitcase. She is disheveled and drained. She sniffles as she meanders in, closing the door behind her. She leaves the suitcase by the coffee table and shuffles over to the kitchen. She pours herself a glass of water, leaves it on the counter and fills a kettle with water from the faucet. She begins boiling water on the stove.*

Zara: Sorry, I'm uh… not my usual jovial self, as you can tell.

> *She wipes her face and blows her nose.*

This weekend didn't turn out like I was expecting. Seems like the news of my publication was overshadowed by something else.

> *She plops on the couch and gazes at the ceiling.*

Who would have known my mother wasn't the only woman in Tata's… in my father's terribly busy life. I didn't know, go figure.

> *She goes over to the stereo and switches on the radio. We hear some instrumental music.*

Seems like I have a half-brother after all. I never… never would have reckoned I'd be in this… I don't know. I don't know why I'm like this… I'm sorry you have to see me this way.

> *We hear the kettle going off. She gets up and pours a cup.*

I couldn't stay there. I had to leave. I had to get away from him and back here. I didn't get around to telling him about my trip to Iowa tomorrow.

> *She takes a sip.*

Well, he's always asked for a grandson. Now he's got the next best thing… and I… I get a sibling out of this.

> *She checks her watch and takes another sip.*

I'm exhausted. So much for Sunday mornings…if you'll excuse me, please.

> *She disappears into the bathroom and slams the door behind.*

<u>Scene 7</u>

> *Lights rise on an empty studio apartment filled with boxes. We see movers carrying Zara's loveseat and coffee table. Zara finishes taping a cardboard box. She looks at the audience.*

Zara: Here we go again… another Sunday morning. Sorry about that. I've been pretty busy these past few weeks. I didn't have time to catch up with you. Seems like that trip to Iowa a while back… that turned out to be quite fruitful. I had to interview for a position on this college campus… all-girls, of course. And when I returned home, I received the offer… Professor of Creative Writing. I like the sound of that. Next thing, I know… I'm packing up and ready to start my next chapter.

A mover comes in and carries away a box.

I never met up again with my father. We spoke on the phone. A little more cordial this time. I'm still not over what happened. I don't think I will be for a while. Will I ever get to meet my new younger brother? I'm certain I will; just don't give me a timetable. I've got bigger plans in store.

A mover comes in and takes away the box she just finished.

All done. My book and record collection are shipped to my new place of residence. You know, I the longer I stayed here in DC, the less attached I became. Every so often, I'll ride my bike past our old Hansel and Gretel style cottage house. I did it yesterday for the last time. I know there's a new family inside. Making new memories, new experiences. I started weirding myself out because I'm watching this going on… I'm not participating. Not moving forward. To think of all those memories I had.

In the kitchen we see a father slow dancing with his infant daughter.

My favorite memory was seeing my Dad arriving back from a long day, while my Mum who would greet him at the door with a glass of wine and a kiss. Now those moments are just… I don't know anymore. I said goodbye to the house, peddled away and sold my bike online this morning.

> *She turns a look at the two of them, before she picks up a bag and exits the apartment. We hear the locking of the door as the father and daughter continue slow dancing. Lights down.*

End of play

Candy from Kenosha

By

John Bolen

John Bolen is a novelist/playwright/actor living in Southern California. He has been published by *Applause Theatre & Cinema Books* three times *(Hal Leonard Publishing), Independentplay(w)rights, Indigo Rising, Scars Publications, The Write Place at the Write Time, OC180news, Eunoia Review* and *YouthPLAYS*. John's plays have been produced in theatres throughout the U.S. including: New Jersey Repertory; Stages Theatre, CA; Chance Theater, CA; Cabrillo Playhouse, CA; Theatre@First, MA; NewGate Theatre, RI; Newport Theatre Arts Center, CA; Thalian Hall Studio Center, NC; Costa Mesa Playhouse, CA; Secret Rose Theatre, CA; The Asylum Theatre, CA; Lincoln Square Theatre, Chicago, IL; Malibu Stage Company, CA; Vanguard Theatre, CA; Garden Grove Playhouse, CA; Red Room Theatre, NYC; Gallery Theatre, CA; Stage Door Repertory, CA; and the Empire Theatre, CA. His short story collection **Nothing for Christmas & Other Holiday Tales** and his novel **Aurelia's Magic** are available on Amazon. As an actor, John has worked on stage, in film and TV, and has recorded 35 books on CD. John is the Vice-President of the New Voices Playwrights Theatre & Workshop.

CHARACTERS

Artie, male, 30's-50's

Helga, female, mid-30s

> *The setting is a topless bar outside Kenosha, WI; the imaginary stages for the dancers are offstage. Artie is behind the bar pouring himself a drink. He grabs a microphone. As he speaks, Helga walks into the bar, setting her purse on a table. She wears a conservative blouse and skirt, more appropriate for church on Sunday than a topless bar.*

Artie: Your eyes on the center pole, gentlemen, as Sin from Cincinnati takes the stage proving Mies van der Rohe's maxim that less is more. Cincinnati's loss is our gain. Give a big hand for this afternoon's star attraction. Watch her and learn what Sin is all about.

> *Artie puts down the mic and speaks to Helga.*

So what's your poison?

Helga: What?

Artie: Drink?... What do you want to drink?

Helga: Oh, nothing.

Artie: If you didn't see the huge sign as you entered, there is a two drink minimum. You want to see the show, you gotta pay the piper.

Helga: Oh, I'm not here to watch the strippers. How could you think that?

Artie: Darling, my partner and I have owned this bar for ten years, and there is nothing that would surprise me now. So are you Five-O? Are you here to bust us? We are just a topless bar. Naked breasts are artistic expression; the Supreme Court has said so. So what else has the Sheriff come up with to try and close us...

Helga: I'm not the police.

Artie: And I should believe you why? You idiots have come at us with every ridiculous...

Helga: I need a job.

> *Artie is suddenly very intrigued; he steps from behind the bar.*

Artie: Really! Well that's a whole other kettle of fish.

Helga: Where are you from, uh...

Artie: Artie, name's Artie.

Helga: I'm Helga. One minute you're quoting Bauhaus philosophy and the next you are using some of the strangest idioms. "Whole other kettle of fish"?

Artie: Would a "whole other ball of wax" be better? And what does a farm woman know of mid-Twentieth Century German Art movements?

Helga: How do you know I'm a farm woman?

Artie: Calluses on your hands and dirt under the fingernails; I grew up on a farm. Those are a dead giveaway.

Helga: Just because I work a farm doesn't mean I am ignorant; Masters degree from Iowa State.

Artie: I see. My parents were immigrants. My father felt the quickest was for us to blend into American society was to speak like Americans speak. Every quirky phrase was drummed into our heads So, how is it you're here pounding the pavement looking for work?

Helga: The tariffs are destroying the markets for our crops, and the bailouts only help giant agribusiness. I have kids to feed. Every other business is hurting when the farms are hurt. You're the only place with a full parking lot. So I'm following the money.

Artie: People make all kinds of judgments about this business; but it is recession proof.

Helga: I'll bartend; I'll sweep the floors; I'll clean the bathrooms; I'll do whatever it...

Artie: My partner and I split up the bartending shifts, and we have an outside service that cleans.

Helga: I'm sorry to waste your...

Artie: What about dancing?

Helga: I won't be made fun of.

Helga grabs her purse and starts to leave.

Artie: I apologize. I wasn't making fun of you, I swear. Please come back.

Helga: I have eyes in my head; I can look at these women here dancing.

Artie: Are you sure about what you see?

Helga: They have skinny little bodies and large breasts. The guys in this place want Playboy and Victoria's Secret models. That is not me. I am no Sin from Cincinnati. I'm plain Helga from Pleasant Prairie, Wisconsin. I've worked a farm my entire life, and my body shows for it. So whatever little joke you're getting out of this, it is not appreciated. I'm ready to clean people's shit if need be. My husband is dead one year, and there are bills to be paid or I'll lose the farm.

Artie: Sorry to hear about your husband.

Helga: He wasn't perfect but he tried. He had a bad heart.

Artie: Every woman has their own story of how they came to be here. Many have children at home; some are paying for school. You know who makes the most money of them all; not the ones who despite my saying over and over again, "It isn't necessary," went out and got boob jobs thinking they will make more money. The girl that makes the most is on stage right now. Six-year-old boys have bigger tits than Claudia.

Helga: So her name isn't really Sin?

Artie: Look at the guys in the front row. They're not drunk; they're respectfully putting down $20 bills on the stage, not trying to stuff them in her bikini bottom. She makes the most with what God gave her. These guys are mostly from the Marine base, in between deployments, far from home and longing for the type of girl they grew up with. They can get all the Playboy models in the world on their computers. So why do they come here? They spend a shitload of money, here. The reason is they are all suffering from the same disease.

Helga: What are you talking about?

Artie: They are suffering from the most debilitating sickness in this world.

Helga: I don't...

Artie: Loneliness. And they will spend every dime they have to try and ease the symptoms.

Helga: This has nothing to do with...

Artie: You could make a lot of money.

Helga: You're crazy.

Artie: I'm very good at what I do, and I'm telling you, they will fall in love with you.

Helga: I've had enough of...

Artie: I'll prove it to you.

Helga: How?

Artie: So if I prove it to you, you'll try dancing for us?

Helga: Oh God, what would they say at church?

Artie: Are they paying your bills?

Helga: The preacher put out a plea for us two Sundays ago during services. We got three lasagnas. Everybody is hurting; I understand it...

Artie: I'm talking about a lot more than three lasagnas.

Helga: I don't think you can prove it to me, so what the hell.

Artie: See the guys in the second row. They are kind of looking this way.

Helga: I see them.

Artie: Unbutton the top button of your blouse.

Helga: What?

Artie: Just one button; no big deal right?

> *Helga nervously unbuttons the button. The guys break out in applause.*

Helga: That doesn't prove...

Artie: Now unbutton the bottom button.

> *Helga looks back at the audience and unbuttons her bottom button. Major cheers break out.*

Helga: Well, maybe...

Artie: No maybe about it.

Helga: I can't do this.

Artie: It wouldn't be forever. Just until the farm is paying off again. Are you worried about how your kids would take it?

Helga: They've been raised that you have to do what's practical. You can't survive on a farm without that understanding. They will be okay.

Artie: So you ready to get naked?

Helga: You're talking about right away?

Artie: No time like the present. I'll put you on the right side stage. Use the pole if you're comfortable with it but if not, just stay in front of it.

Helga: I'll be too nervous.

Artie: That will pass once you're up there. You're not wearing granny panties are you?

Helga: No.

Artie: You are wearing some kind of panties, right?

Helga: Yes. Is that what this is all about? Are you trying to have sex with me?

Artie: Well, there would be a big problem with that.

Helga: What's that?

Artie: You weren't born with the right equipment.

Helga: Oh? Oh!

Artie: But as long as we're on the topic, no tricks on the property, and not even making dates.

Helga: Tricks? Oh!

Artie: We are legit; no screwing around. So get on stage. I'll introduce you.

Helga: Uhhh...

Artie: What?

Helga: What name are you going to use for me?

Artie: You don't want to be Helga from Pleasant Prairie?

Helga: No, I have to be someone else.

Artie: I'll agree, but only if you promise that in every way you'll just be yourself. You are beautiful, and that's what they want to see. So what name are you going to use?

Helga: I don't know. Lola from Lake Shangrila?

Artie: Maybe a little too cheesy. Can we use Kenosha, so they know you're a local woman?

Helga: I guess.

Artie: How about Candy from Kenosha? Just as sweet as she can be.

Helga: Yeah, that's good.

Artie: So are you ready?

Helga: What if they hate me?

Artie: Trust me, they won't. We're going to have to expand the parking lot.

Helga: This is all so unexpected.

Artie: That you would find yourself dancing?

Helga: That you would be so nice; thank you, Artie.

Artie: Come on, get out there. Make money for us.

Helga runs up and hugs Artie. Artie moves behind the bar. As the music comes up, Artie grabs the mic.

Helga: This is so crazy.

Artie: Not at all. We all do what we gotta do.

Helga: What do I do?

Artie: Just look in their eyes and smile.

Helga heads off stage towards the imaginary stage.

(Into the mic.) All right, Gentlemen, I turn your attention to stage number two, where we have the debut of a local lady, who, as she just told me, spends every night just thinking of you. I suspect, after today, you will spend every night thinking of her. Let's have a big cheer for Candy from Kenosha. This is the kind of Candy you will get a real sweet tooth for.

A big cheer and applause is heard.

End of play.

Four Characters in Search of a Play

By

John Lane

Four Characters in Search of a Play was first produced at the Stage Door Repertory Theatre in June 2013, directed by Katherine Scott and starred Elizabeth Desloge, Ian Downs, Jonathon Lamer and Gloria Maxwell.

John Lane is a former professor at Cal-State Long Beach who took up an avocation of playwriting after being a long-time theatre fan. He took courses at South Coast Repertory in Costa Mesa, California and sitcom writing at AFI in Los Angeles. He is a member of two playwriting groups in Orange County: New Voices and Orange County Playwrights Alliance. He is a founding member and former president of New Voices. He is also a member of the Dramatists Guild. In the past 20 years about 40 of his short plays have been produced in California and nationally, including six productions in New York City. Although his specialty is comedy, he has written some serious dramas as well. One of his long one-act plays, **Isosceles,** was performed at the OC-centric Festival at Chapman University in Orange California.

CHARACTERS

Constance, female, 60s-70s, family matriarch

Beth, female, 20s-30s, daughter of Constance

Farnsworth, male 30s-30s, a possibly corrupt doctor

Nigel, male, 30s-40s, Constance's son, and coincidentally, Beth's brother

> *Constance is in a hospital bed. She is propped up and chatting with Beth.*

Constance*:* Where is Nigel? I won't let anyone feed me except Nigel.

Beth: For God's sake, Mother. Nigel hasn't been here for months. As you know, since leaving the university to finish his book, his wife Francesca has been having an affair with the head of the Theatre Arts department, Tyson Manbait, whom everyone thought was gay. But really, he's just someone who likes opera, ballet, and macramé. *(Beat.)* The last we heard from Nigel, he was in Duluth.

Constance: Why are you telling me things I already know? Except that part about Duluth. Why would someone go to Duluth in January?

Beth: *(Grandly.)* Nigel needs the isolation. He feels isolation is the mother's milk of inspiration which irrigates the sands of time.

Constance: Really, Beth! We spent thousands getting you an English degree at Wellesley, and you're still mixing your metaphors. *(Looks around.)* Who the devil is going to feed me?

Beth: Mother, there's nothing wrong with your motor skills. You're quite capable of feeding yourself. In fact, there's no reason for you to be in this hospital.

Constance: I get the attention here that I deserve. Ever since Cosmo, my husband, died, I've been clinically depressed. And lest you forget, Cosmo is also the father of my son, Nigel.

Beth: I'm quite aware of that, Mother, since Nigel is my brother and Cosmo is also my father. Why do you feel the need to dwell on these relationships?

Constance: Exposition, my dear; exposition. *(Beat.)* Dr. Farnsworth tells me I'm depressed.

Beth: For the record, Mother, you are not clinically depressed, you are just down in the dumps and feeling blue. I told Dr. Farnsworth to cut off your meds.

Constance: See here, Missy, since when do you tell Dr. Farnsworth what to prescribe? I trust Dr. Farnsworth above all others. He alone knows what's best for me.

Beth: Farnsworth is a pompous ass and is obviously after your money. What's more, his medical degree is from Australia, but there is no record of his ever having been in Australia.

Constance: His never having been is Australia is easily explained; he's had a lifelong fear of emus. He dreads an emu flying in his face.

Beth: I believe the Emu is a flightless bird.

Constance: Nevertheless, Dr. Farnsworth chose to err on the side of discretion. He avoids Australia at all costs.

> *Farnsworth enters.*

Farnsworth: Good morning, ladies.

Constance: *(Gushing.)* Oh, Dr. Farnsworth!

Beth: *(Sullenly.)* Hello, Farnsworth.

Farnsworth: *(Confidentially.)* Beth, could I talk with you privately?

> *Beth and Farnsworth move away from Constance for privacy.*

Farnsworth: *(Aside, to Beth.)* I really feel we must keep Constance, I mean your mother, here another month.

Beth: There's no need for that. My mother is perfectly well.

Farnsworth: Constance, that is your mother, is down in the dumps; I would even say depressed.

Constance: *(Loudly.)* I can hear everything you two are saying.

Beth: For God's sake, Mother, it's an <u>aside</u>. Pretend you don't hear us. You have to follow the rules. Did it occur to you, Farnsworth, that Mother is down in the dumps due to this deplorably dark, joyless hospital room?

Farnsworth: The hospital board is trying to control costs. Did you know that by not installing windows, they saved over eighty-thousand dollars?

Beth: You can't put monetary value on everything, Farnsworth; although, eighty thousand is a tidy sum.

Farnsworth: I've persuaded Constance, that is, your mother, to make a sizeable donation to my charitable foundation. Using my foundation, her money can be used to help the less fortunate.

Beth: Your foundation is a sham. When Nigel, my brother, arrives, he will certainly challenge you on that.

Farnsworth: I thought Nigel, your brother, was in Duluth finishing his book.

Beth: He returned early, since he discovered his wife having an affair with the head of the Theatre Arts department, Tyson Manbait.

Farnsworth: Are you quite sure? I thought Manbait was gay. After all, he does like opera, ballet and macramé.

Beth: Manbait was fiendishly clever about all that. Naturally, no one suspected him of having an affair with a woman, much less Nigel's wife, Francesca.

>*Nigel enters; inexplicably, he has a British accent.*

Nigel: Did someone mention Francesca?

Beth: My God, Nigel, it's you!

Nigel: I bloody well know it's me.

Constance: Nigel, thank God, you're just in time to feed me.

Nigel: Feed you, Mother? What are you talking about? You're quite capable of feeding yourself. What have you been telling her, Farnsworth?

Farnsworth: Nigel, your mother Constance must stay here another month. She is quite depressed.

Nigel: Stuff and nonsense, Farnsworth; she's never looked better.

Constance: Oh, Nigel, my favorite child, you are the only one I trust. But why do you insist on that British accent? You were born in New Jersey.

Beth: You always did favor Nigel, Mother. It's no wonder I've turned to a life of drink and joyless sex. But at least I thought you trusted me.

Farnsworth: I also thought you trusted me, Constance. After all, you're making a sizable contribution to my foundation so the less fortunate can be looked after.

Beth: Really, Farnsworth, you are only interested in looking after yourself. Spare us the pathos.

Nigel: I'm sure this "foundation" of yours is headquartered in some shady tax shelter offshore.

Farnsworth: My foundation is headquartered in Australia, if you call that offshore.

Nigel: But you've never been in Australia; although strangely, your medical degree is from the University of Melbourne.

Farnsworth: I fear I would get disoriented if I lived in Australia. Down there they drive in the other side of the road, water swirls down the drain in the reverse direction, you can't see the North Star, and the seasons are backward. Not to mention the inherent dangers of a large emu population. My foundation is headquartered there solely for tax considerations.

Constance: Dr. Farnsworth tells me that his foundation will look after the less fortunate.

Nigel: Have you been overmedicating my mother, Farnsworth? She is quite incoherent at times.

Farnsworth: Coherence is very much overrated. They called Isaac Einstein incoherent when he invented the space-time continuum.

Nigel: Farnsworth, I want you to release my mother from this hospital immediately. *(Beat.)* And by the way, I have reconciled with Francesca.

Beth: Thank God, we need to advance that subplot.

Constance: Now what will become of Tyson Manbait, Francesca's gay, illicit lover and head of the Theatre Arts department? They say he loves opera, ballet, and macramé.

Beth: You're thinking in stereotypes, Mother. Everyone who likes macramé is not gay.

Farnsworth: Your mother remains down in the dumps. I cannot in good conscience release her, Nigel.

Nigel: Balderdash, Farnsworth, you never had a conscience. And that phony degree of yours from the University of Melbourne fools no one.

Farnsworth: Your mother needs intensive treatment for the blues. I am bringing in a licensed therapeutic clown.

Constance: Heavens, no! I'm terrified of clowns. They have bulbous noses and gigantic eyes and are sometimes very sad.

Farnsworth: Nonsense, how can anyone be afraid of clowns?

Beth: How can anyone be afraid of emus?

Farnsworth: There is no need for cruel sarcasm, Beth.

Nigel: Francesca and I have booked a charming hotel in the Bahamas to celebrate our reconciliation.

Beth: How will you finish your book? Don't you need isolation?

Nigel: Isolation is very much overrated. In point of fact, I did my best work on my laptop in a crowded Starbucks.

Farnsworth: *(Perhaps facing the audience.)* Let me see if I have this straight. Nigel and Francesca are reconciled. Constance is afraid of clowns. I have a foundation that purports to aid the less fortunate but Beth questions my medical degree and fears I have duped her mother into investing in this same foundation.

Beth: Bor—ing! Exposition is highly overrated.

Constance: Where is Francesca? It seems we never get to see her.

Nigel: Don't be daft, Mother; four characters are quite enough for a short play. She must remain an offstage presence. After all, there are budgetary considerations.

Farnsworth: You can't put a monetary value on art.

Beth: How ironic coming from you, Farnsworth. You put a monetary value on everything!

Constance sniffles into a handkerchief.

Nigel: Mother, why are you crying?

Constance: I do miss my Cosmo.

Farnsworth: I told you she was depressed. *(Beat.)* Who the devil is Cosmo?

Nigel: He is Mother's husband, my father, and coincidentally the father of my sister, Beth.

Farnsworth: How is it that Cosmo never visits Constance? After all, he is her husband.

Nigel: He is dead, you ninny. So how could he possibly show his face, except perhaps in a flashback scene?

Beth: The cast size must be kept at four for obvious monetary reasons. Besides that, I hate flashbacks.

Constance: It was said that my late husband, Cosmo, Nigel's father, was a mob boss, but I never believed it.

Nigel: Really, Mother, how could you be so naïve? His name is Cosmo Magdalini and he was Sicilian. How do you suppose he became a multi-millionaire operating a small pizza parlor which was notorious as a hangout for the DiAngelo family? And why do you suppose his bullet riddled body was found in a shallow grave outside of Las Vegas?

Constance: They said he died in a bizarre hunting accident.

Beth: Oh God, more exposition. Bor—ing!

Farnsworth: On the contrary, I find all this interesting. Not to mention that it adds considerable subtext to out otherwise rather trite dialogue.

Nigel's cell phone rings.

Nigel: Excuse me. (*He answers phone.*) Francesca, what are you saying... You're back with Tyson? You are going with him to Milan? La Scala? But you've always hated opera. (*Pause.*) Maybe it's just as well. At least I can finish my book... Goodbye, Francesca. (*He hangs up phone.*) That was Francesca. She's back with Tyson and going with him to Milan.

Beth: For God's sake, Nigel, we have ears. Must you repeat everything?

Nigel: How can Francesca be so cruel!? Doesn't she realize I've already paid for four nights at a small charming hotel in the Bahamas, and Priceline doesn't give refunds?

Constance: My Cosmo never liked Francesca.

Nigel: Father never liked strong women. Why do you think he married you, Mother?

Farnsworth: No need to be cruel, Nigel. Cosmo, your father, earned millions as a mob boss. But those millions can now be funneled into my foundation to help the needy. How's that for irony?

Nigel: Irony is a powerful theatrical device, Farnsworth. But you foundation remains a scam.

Beth: I suggest we resolve all these problems. Otherwise, this play will become a tedious one-act.

Nigel: I have retained the services of a solicitor to look into Farnsworth's affairs.

Constance: They are called Lawyers over here, Nigel. Why must you pretend to be English?

Farnsworth: My affairs? What I do in my private life is no concern of yours, Nigel. *(Beat.)* I can't believe that girl was only fourteen.

Nigel: I was referring to your financial affairs, you ninny. Records show your "Foundation" has not paid taxes for the past five years. Not to mention that it maintains a private jet for your frequent trips to Hawaii, Tahiti and Malta.

Farnsworth: Of course, I require a jet. How did you expect me to get to Hawaii, Tahiti and Malta? Swim? If you'd take the trouble to consult an atlas, you would find they are all islands.

Nigel: Also, the foundation maintains a villa for you in Naples.

Constance: *(Reminisces.)* I love Naples. Cosmo took me there on our honeymoon. There's an old Italian saying, "See Naples and die!" And now my Cosmo is dead. *(Sobs.)* It's a Sicilian curse.

Beth: Why do you need a villa in Naples, Farnsworth? I suppose you would say, to help the needy and less fortunate?

Farnsworth: Spare me your sarcasm, Beth, although sarcasm can be an effective theatrical device.

Nigel: This clever scam of yours is over, Farnsworth. Federal agents are on their way here as we speak. The FBI has been preparing a case against you for months.

Constance: *(Reminisces again.)* The Feds caught Cosmo for income tax evasion, just like Al Capone. Cosmo was very proud of that. He considered Capone a role model.

Beth: Fortunately, Mother, your sizable donation to Farnsworth's foundation can be recovered. We can stop payment on the check.

Farnsworth: You're too late, Beth. Constance's check has already cleared. But her sizable donation can still help the needy. I am, of course, referring to myself. I am in dire need of a top-notch lawyer.

Nigel: Say goodbye to your villa in Naples, Farnsworth. You will now be spending your time in another villa... near the California coast... it's called San Quentin. Your cell may have a view. They say on a clear day, you can see the guard towers.

>*There is a loud knock on the door.*

The Feds are here! It's the end of the road for you, Farnsworth.

Beth: At last, I have the pleasure of watching this charlatan Farnsworth getting arrested.

Nigel: Actually, you won't see the actual arrest. The play has to end now. If those Feds come in, we're stuck paying three actors for lousy bit parts that would put us over budget.

The loud knocks continue.

Constance: For God's sake, Nigel, open the door for them.

Nigel: After the blackout, Mother. Right after the blackout.

Blackout, followed by further loud knocks.

End of play.

Going Up

By

Pattric Walker

Pattric Walker is a musician, song writer, playwright, director, actor, and artist currently living and working in Southern California.   Of her plays that have been produced, she considers the world premiere of her full-length drama, *Dragons in New York* at the acclaimed Chance Theatre in Anaheim Hills her highest achievement so far. In addition to plays, her book *33 Ways to Shape Up Your Slim Down*, various cartoons, poetry, and editorials have appeared in popular publications. Pattric's plays have been published in previous editions of *New Voices Playwrights' Annual Anthology of Short Plays,* and *New Voices Holiday Plays*.

CHARACTERS

Stan, male, mid-20's to early 30's, works out, in great shape, muscular but not like a male stripper or lifter, boyfriend to Charlene.

Charlene, female, 20's to early 30's, junior designer at an architectural firm.

Millicent, female, late-20's to early-30's, junior designer at an architectural firm.

Mr. Gibbs, male, 55+, Senior Partner and founder of Gibbs & Dunn.

> *The large freight elevator at Gibbs & Dunn, an architectural firm. At rise, Charlene and Stan enter, stop at the elevator. Charlene carries a large, flat, priority mail envelope.*

Stan: Are you sure this is a good idea? You know how I get.

Charlene: You can do this, Stan. The freight elevator goes directly down to the mail room. It will be quick. I want to get this out today. Mr. Gibbs will be making his final decision in a few days, and I want him to have plenty of time to go over my plans. If they arrive late, he may not even look at them.

> *Stan pushes the call button.*

Stan: Late is what we're going to be if this elevator doesn't come soon. I have a special night planned for tonight.

Charlene: Yes, I know.

Stan: You can't know. How do you know?

Charlene: You show up wearing creased slacks, a starched button down, a jacket, and you think, after three years with you, I'm not going to notice? I'm lucky when you put on pants. This is like winning the lottery.

Stan: Hold that thought.

Stan pushes call button over and over again.

Charlene: Calm down. It will get here.

Stan: As soon as you drop that off, I'm going to whisk you away so you can forget about that new lab joint.

Charlene: That lab joint is going to be a combination hospital, specialty post-graduate school, and research facility that takes up four city blocks. It will be the biggest and most important medical facility in this state's history. There's a preliminary committee to review all submissions, cut them down to three. Those three will be presented to the developers to decide which firm gets the contract. It's a bit more than a lab joint.

Stan: So, let Gibbs and Dunn worry about it.

Charlene: I'm worried about it. I think it's a test. Projects like this aren't assigned to junior designers; especially not new ones. I won't be able to think of anything else until my drawings are accepted or rejected. If they're rejected, I may be out of a job. I believe I'm a good architect. It would be great if someone else thought that, too.

Stan: You know I do. Besides, you're not new.
You've been here four years.

Charlene: To Gibbs & Dunn, I'm still an infant. Take
Millicent. She walked out of MIT straight into Gibbs &
Dunn's front door. Do you realize what that means?
Super talent. Almost seven years later, she's still a
junior designer.   What does that tell you?

Stan: They like her work?

> *Elevator clunks to a stop, dings, and doors
> open.*

Charlene: Finally.

> *Charlene enters first, then, as Stan starts to
> enter, Millicent calls out.*

Millicent: *(Offstage.)* Wait!

> *Millicent enters quickly, carrying a huge
> priority mail box with a tall design model
> peeking out of the top.*

Millicent: Wait!

> *Stan holds elevator doors open.*

Charlene: *(To Stan.)* What are you doing? She's my
competition.

Stan: What?

> *Millicent enters elevator.*

Millicent: *(Polite, to a co-worker.)* Thank you. Oh,
hello, Charlene.

Charlene: Millicent, this is my boyfriend, Stan. Stan, this is the other junior designer I was telling you about.

Millicent: Were you?

Stan: *(Trying to get doors to close.)* Hired right out of MIT. A super talent, I'm told. *(Takes off his jacket.)* Hi. These are really stuck. *(Back to un-sticking doors.)*

Millicent: Looks like we're all going to the mail room. Interesting.

> *Charlene looks at the model poking out of the top of the box Millicent is holding.*

Charlene: Not as interesting as that.

Millicent: Oh. You're my competition. No one would tell me who it was.

Stan: It has to be somebody, right?

> *Charlene and Millicent give Stan a look.*

Stan: Right. Not my business.

> *Stan takes off his shirt, has on a wife-beater, works out, with great results. Millicent notices, quickly catches herself, returns to neutral.*

Millicent: *(To Stan, referring to discarded shirt.)* What are you doing?

> *Stan is without words, fighting anxiety.*

Charlene: *(Covering for Stan.)* I'm a little warm. It's getting hot in here.

Stan: Yes, it's getting hot in here. Carry on. *(Back to un-sticking doors.)*

Millicent: What is it you do, Stan?

Stan: *(Proudly.)* I count fish.

Millicent: As you said, it has to be somebody, doesn't it?

Stan: Hey, you get it.

Millicent: *(To Charlene.)* I'm assuming those are your design plans.

Charlene: And that's your model. You've put in a lot of work.

> *A big screech as the elevator doors close.*

Stan: *(Anxiety escalating.)* It is hot in here. *(Takes off his tee shirt.)*

Millicent: Yes, it is getting hot isn't it.

> *Millicent sets down box, takes off jacket, and unbuttons top buttons of blouse. Stan takes off his shoes and socks and notices Millicent noticing.*

Stan: I'm used to working on a trawler. If it bothers you, I'll...

Millicent: *(Looking at Stan's chest, then quickly switching.)* I've seen bare feet before.

> *Elevator comes to a thudding halt, lights go out.*

Charlene: No. This can't happen. Not now.

Stan: Oh, oh, oh.

Charlene: Stan? You're not, are you? Please tell me you aren't. You can't. Not here.

Stan: Honey, I'm sorry. I can't help it.

Charlene: *(Feeling around.)* Stan, no, please! Where are you?

Millicent: Who is that? Take your hand off my breast.

Charlene: Sorry, Millicent.

Stan: *(Finds Charlene and pulls her toward him.)* I'm over here, Charlene.

> *Emergency lights come on, brighter than the mood lights. Stan is naked, Charlene standing in front of him, blocking him. Millicent takes one look; turns around to the wall.*

Charlene: Millicent, I'm sorry. Stan is a little claustrophobic.

Stan: Come on, Charlene. I'm a lot claustrophobic. I can't stand to wear clothes. I'm a nudist.

Charlene: Millicent, you look uncomfortable. Are you all right?

Millicent: I'm fine, just fine. If you call counting grain lines in phony walnut fine. Tell him to put his clothes back on.

> *Charlene feels Stan's tension, turns around just in time to plant the large envelope in front of*

> *Stan's essentials to cover them as Stan steps*
> *forward from behind Charlene.*

Stan: It's hot in here. I'm claustrophobic, and I'm doing my best to fight off a serious meltdown. You have no idea what it took for me to put those clothes on in the first place. I did it for Charlene, but I can only go so far. So shoot me. I have issues.

Charlene: Sweetheart, you're doing so well. You made a huge effort, and I love you all the more for it.

> *Charlene, Stan share little kisses, hands free*
> *since Stan has to hold the envelope in place.*

Millicent: Stop it, stop it, stop it! This is not a porn in the box. If you want love in an elevator...

Stan: Aerosmith. One of my favorite songs. Are you a rocker, too?

Millicent: Is he always like this?

Charlene: Pretty much. That's why I love him.

Millicent: You can explain it to me later. Does he let you dress him?

Stan: I'll get dressed when we get saved.

Millicent: There's an uplifting turn of phrase. Charlene, help me out here. Can't you do something?

Stan: We could all relax. Just turn around.

Charlene/Millicent: No!

Charlene: Oh, Millicent, I'm sorry. I should have told you. Stan is covered. You can turn around.

Millicent: All of him? He's put his clothes back on?

Stan: I can't do that.

Charlene: Wait, I know what we can do.

> *Charlene takes the model out of the large box, opens the bottom, hands it to Stan.*

Charlene: Put this on.

Stan: How is this any different than...

Charlene: Put it on!

Stan: All right, already. Um, I only have one hand.

> *Charlene holds the box open so Stan can step into it, then lifts the box and, at the appropriate moment, the box replaces the envelope Stan lifts out of the way with no peek-a-boo moment.*

Charlene: It is hot. *(Takes off her blouse.)* It's safe now. Stan can even walk around.

Millicent: *(Spins around quickly.)* What do you mean walk...?

> *Millicent stops dead when she sees Stan, who does a full turn, like a model, to show he's fully covered. Millicent laughs.*

Stan: What's so funny?

Millicent: This. I've been so focused on my work, the model, my future, and now, this, us, like this.

> *Charlene, Stan join in the laughter, more nervous and awkward than funny, a release.*

> *Millicent takes off her blouse and skirt, exposing lacy undies and bra, garter belt and stockings, and an outstanding figure Stan notices. So does Charlene.*

Charlene: What do you think you're doing?

Millicent: The same as you, apparently, staying cooler. *(Kicks off her heels.)* Much better. I wonder how long we'll be stuck.

Charlene: He's my boyfriend. I can get naked if I want. Not you.

Millicent: He got naked first. *(A bit flirty, to Stan.)* So will I, if it means not dying in here.

Stan: *(Flirting back.)* You won't die even if you do get naked. It's liberating.

Millicent: Maybe. It'll consider it if we're forgotten and going to die. Until then, this is all you're going to get.

Stan: That looks pretty cool.

Charlene: *(To Millicent.)* What do you think you're doing? *(To Stan.)* And you!

Stan: Call it survival. I say we all get naked. *(Starts to drop the box.)*

Charlene/Millicent: No!

Charlene: *(Puts her hands on Stan's to hold the box.)* Behave yourself.

Millicent: We all have our little foibles.

Charlene picks up the model.

Charlene: This is magnificent. Some of these design elements are inspired.

Millicent: You like it? Really?

Stan: Wow, this is really something.

Millicent: I appreciate that, Charlene. I've always admired your work.

Charlene: You have?

Millicent: May I see your designs?

Charlene: You mean the litter on the floor?

Stan: Sometimes, even litter, like fallen leaves, can make a beautiful pattern. You just have to look for the beauty.

Millicent: *(To Charlene, indicating Stan.)* Grows on you?

Charlene: Like a wild passion flower vine.

Stan: I'm naked, not deaf.

Charlene: *(To Millicent.)* It isn't fair, really, to exclude him. Considering… *(Indicates the stuck elevator.)*

Charlene/Millicent: We're sorry.

> *Charlene gets envelope, unfolds blueprints and drawings, holds them for Millicent to view.*

Millicent: This is Arches heavy bond water color paper. Highly absorbent. If we need to go to the…

Stan: No you won't. Not on her designs, you won't.

Millicent: Yes. Yes, you're right. They're too valuable. *(Looks around.)* My suit is Armani. *(To Stan.)* We can use your suit.

> *Stan wants to snap back, stops himself, steps over to look at the designs.*

Millicent: *(Pointing out to Charlene.)* Look, here. We were on the same track. There are only minor differences.

Stan: It's set wrong.

> *Charlene and Millicent look at Stan.*

Millicent: *(To Charlene.)* Counts fish.

Charlene: Department of Wildlife and Fisheries. One of their best. *(To Stan.)* Something you'd like to say?

Stan: Get the model for me, I can show you.

Charlene: Can't you get the model yourself?

Stan: Glad to, if that's what you want. I'm tired of holding up this box.

Charlene/Millicent: No!

Charlene: *(Sets down plans, kisses Stan on her way by.)* I'll get it, honey.

Stan: I thought you might, sweetheart.

> *Charlene holds up the model as Stan explains, Millicent paying close attention.*

Stan: I'll be North. *(To Charlene.)* Turn it a quarter turn. This is how you have the buildings set now. Why?

Millicent: I want the largest banks of windows to face the water, for the view.

Stan: That's your windward side. You'll get your view, but it'll cost you. High heating costs, more rust and corrosion, shorter materials life span, more frequent maintenance, all kinds of problems with wind. Plus, you could have a water run-off issue. *(To Charlene.)* One more quarter turn, please.

Charlene turns the model.

Stan: What is the view turned this way?

Millicent: Marsh land, mostly, water in the distance.

Stan: So, there would be birds, rivulets, greenery; maybe fishermen to watch. See, if this building was faced this way, and you took this corner and made it a wrap around, curved stair case or something, you could still get the full view, but with a wall that will let the wind wrap around it instead of slamming into it. Your run-off would be better absorbed into the marsh land off the parking lot, too, I think. I'm not the experts. You are.

Millicent: I should have gotten better people to do my research, or done it myself. *(To Charlene.)* Your drawings are different on that side aren't they? *(Picks up Charlene's drawings.)*

Charlene: Yes, see how I have the windows tilted back into the building on the bottom? I was hoping the extra overhang and directing the wind down would mitigate the long term effects flat-facing windows would have. But, I made the same mistake you did. We both went for the view.

Stan: Hey, don't call it a mistake because of what I said. I count fish.

Millicent: On the sea, in the wind, day after day. I believe you're right. That building needs to be redirected. Maybe this is the hand of Fate. *(To Charlene.)* Do you think we'll get our designs to Mr. Gibbs by the deadline?

Charlene: We'll lose today for sure. The deadline is in three days... Funny, I'd forgotten about that.

Stan: Good to hear. I don t want you to be distracted tonight.

Millicent: Tonight? An optimist are you, Stan?

Stan: Why not?

Millicent: Why not indeed. Charlene, have you ever considered having your own firm?

Charlene: No, why?

Millicent: I won't lie to you, Charlene. This is it for me. If this doesn't get me a promotion, I'm leaving Gibbs & Dunn.

Charlene: What about all the time you've put in?

Millicent: That's what it feels like, Charlene. Doing time. I won't do it again. I don t intend to start

somewhere else as a junior designer, and I don't want
to go into business by myself. I want other talented
eyes to review my work, make sure I haven't become
too egotistical to think I can't make mistakes.
Obviously, I can. I did, on this. I want eyes and talent,
like yours.

Charlene: You want me to go into business with you?

Stan: Why not?

Charlene: Who asked you?

Stan: I think it's a great idea.

Millicent: So, Stan, you have big plans for Charlene
tonight, do you?

Stan: I did.

Millicent: I wish you well with those.

> *Stan starts to extend his hand to shake,
> forgetting about the box, quickly catches it.*

Stan: Oh, jeez. Got it! Thanks, Millicent. You know
what? I think you're all right.

Millicent: Back at ya, Stan. One rocker to another. *(To
Charlene.)* You don't have to decide right now.

Stan: Leave it up in the air?

Millicent: Up. Yes, keep thinking up. Anything but
down. I wonder what floor we're on.

Mr. Gibbs: *(Offstage.)* Hello? *(Enters.)* Hello?
Anybody down here?

Charlene/Millicent: We're in here! The elevator! Can you hear us? In here!

Mr. Gibbs: Yes, yes, I hear you. Hang on. We'll get you out. *(Steps to the side of the elevator doors to make walkie-talkie call.)* Hello? Yes, there are people trapped in an elevator on Basement One, the mail room. Do I have to call the fire dep... Oh, you can? Remotely. Then, please do. *(Holds walkie-talkie away from ear, watches elevator doors, straining, but not opening. Then, into walkie-talkie.)* They're not opening... What? All right, just a minute.   Hello? Inside the elevator. Can you hear me?

Charlene/Millicent: Yes. Yes, we can hear you.

Mr. Gibbs: The elevator doors are stuck.

> *Charlene, Millicent share a, "Tell us something we don't know," look. Stan is amused.*

Mr. Gibbs: Can you help get them open from the inside?

Charlene/Millicent: Yes.

Stan: *(As he steps toward the doors.)* Ladies, I could use some assistance or would you rather I... *(Fakes starting to let go of the box.)*

Charlene/Millicent: No!

> *Millicent catches one side of the box to hold up, Charlene the other.*

Millicent: Ready.

Mr. Gibbs: All, right. Wait for a count of three, then on three. Just a minute. *(Into walkie-talkie.)* We're going on a count of three. One, two, three.

> *Stan pulls, the doors shriek, then open.*
> *Millicent peeks out and sees Mr. Gibbs.*

Millicent: We may still have time to get our projects in. This is the mail room.

> *Charlene turns to pick up her designs, folds*
> *them neatly. Millicent seizes opportunity, exits,*
> *quickly strides like a model to Mr. Gibbs. Stan*
> *watches.*

Millicent: *(Fully composed, but in a rapid flurry.)* Mr. Gibbs, how nice to see you again. You may not remember me. We met, almost seven years ago, at my interview. I'm a junior designer. Millicent Caulfield. *(Extends hand to shake.)*

> *Mr. Gibbs shakes as Millicent races on.*

Millicent: I'm one of the two junior designers tasked with presenting you with proposed designs for the hospital research lab project. I was on my way to send my design to you, but as long as you're here… Just give me a minute. I'll get my model.

Mr. Gibbs: You work for me?

> *Millicent quickly returns to the elevator to get*
> *her model, as Charlene is just as quickly*
> *heading toward Mr. Gibbs.*

Charlene: *(To Millicent.)* Nice going. Partner.

Millicent: I'm not out of here yet. A girl's got to do what a girl's got to do. Right, Stan?

Stan: You bet.

> *Charlene turns to harrumph at Stan, then turns to Mr. Gibbs, rushing, knowing Millicent will soon return.*

Charlene: Mr. Gibbs, how very nice to meet you. I'm Charlene Cavanaugh, a junior designer. The other junior designer tasked to present you with plans for the lab jo...

Stan: Uh, uh, uh.

Charlene: The laboratory project. *(Thrusts her drawings into Mr. Gibbs's hands.)* I think you'll find these to your liking. There is a modification I'm going to want to make. I'm sure you'll see the benefit of the change.

> *Millicent comes striding up, hands her model to Mr. Gibbs, who awkwardly takes it.*

Millicent: As do I. The modification is not extensive and only involves one corner of a building. I'm sure it won't deter you from appreciating the entire design.

> *Stan, holding the box, can't applaud, so he stomps his feet instead, a huge smile on his face. Millicent, Charlene, Mr. Gibbs look at him.*

Mr. Gibbs: Does he work for me, too?

Charlene: No sir. He's my boyfriend. He counts fish.

Millicent: On a trawler.

> *Millicent and Charlene look at each other,
> decide on a hasty retreat.*

Charlene/Millicent: *(Backing up.)* Thank you, Mr. Gibbs.

Millicent: *(To Charlene.)* Slowly, hold up our heads.

> *Mr. Gibbs, holding the model and the
> blueprints, looks at Stan.*

Stan: It was hot in there.

> *Millicent and Charlene stop when they hear
> Stan speak to Mr. Gibbs. Stan crosses to Mr.
> Gibbs, who resists the urge to run.*

Stan: If you'll store my clothes somewhere, maybe Charlene s office, I'd appreciate it. They're the only dress clothes I own. I was going to wear them tonight, but they're probably wrinkled now, so...

Charlene: Stan.

Mr. Gibbs: I'll see what I can do.

Stan: Great, thank you. *(Crosses to Charlene and Millicent.)* Charlene, don't forget, we have reservations for dinner.

Charlene: *(To Millicent.)* He did catch the flaw in our designs. A consultant, maybe?

Millicent: Oh, now we're partners?

Stan: *(To Charlene.)* You decided? Great. Something else to celebrate. Hey, why don't I invite Millicent, too?

Charlene: I'm not sure we have a choice any more.

Mr. Gibbs: Excuse me. I should tell you, the building was evacuated. Everyone is grouped outside. Perhaps you'd like me to arrange some transportation for you? It's turned into somewhat of a press event. You could dress while we're waiting.

> *Millicent, Charlene, and Stan look at each other.*

Millicent: Heads up, proud to be members of Gibbs & Dunn. Designs presented on time.

Charlene: Compatible designs, with the same flaw.

> *Millicent and Charlene look at Mr. Gibbs, then the exit, then the elevator, then at each other.*

Charlene/Millicent: We can do it.

Stan: All engines full ahead?

Charlene: Full ahead.

Millicent: Caulfield & Cavanaugh. We're in business! Stan, when we get to a crest where you can look out over the waves and waves of people, drop your box.

Charlene: Are you sure about that? What about the publicity?

Millicent: Priceless. Our brand will become known overnight.

> *Millicent and Charlene proudly exit. Stan starts to exit then turns to Mr. Gibbs.*

Stan: I hope it isn't really cold out there. *(Exits.)*

> *Mr. Gibbs's s walkie-talkie squawks. He sets
> down model and designs, then answers. He
> looks down on the model more carefully,
> somewhat distracted from the call.*

Mr. Gibbs: Yes, what is it?... Go up? Of course I want to go up. I own this building. Why else do you think my office is on the top floor? Are you sure it's safe?... Just in case, have a crew there to get me out if I do get stuck. Hold on. Wait a minute. *(Carefully looking at model.)* Find my assistant. Tell her to get me the files on Caulfield and Cavanaugh, junior designers, and get them back in here. And find out who's in charge of our dress code. I want to see him or her, now!

<u>End of play.</u>

How Sweet It Is

By

Anne V. Grob

How Sweet It Is serves as a prequel to Anne's play ***How To Have A Kosher*** Christmas which appeared in NV Holiday Show December 2014.

Anne V. Grob, an award winning playwright residing in SoCal, learned her craft at South Coast Repertory's Playwriting Conservatory. She has produced her plays in NYC's Players Theatre SPFs June 2013-2019 and October 2019. *Hemingway at the Larchmont, Once Upon A Sofa, The Bard of MacDougal Street, Alexa Takes Manhattan* and *Used Heart* won best of festival for their performance week. *Mouse Play* appeared in Ohlone College Playwrights Festival 2016, *UNTITLED* placed as finalist and *The Planting Moon* as semi-finalist in Heartland Theatre (2016) and Little Black Dress Ink (2014) festivals, respectively. For New Voices, productions of Anne's work include: *Variations On A Composition In Blue* (Summer, 2014), *How To Have A Kosher Christmas* (Holiday, 2014), *The Trouble With Art* (Summer 2015), *Pentimento* (Summer, 2016), *The Secret Chord* (Holiday, 2016), *Not Even The Moon* (Summer, 2017), *Some Simple Kindness* (Holiday, 2017), *The XYZ of It* (Summer, 2018), *A Cup O' Kindness* (Holiday, 2018), *G.O.A.T., or Who is Alexa?* (Summer, 2019), and *Concerto For Violin* (Holiday, 2019). Anne's plays appear in New Voices Playwrights Theatre anthologies, and *Variations On A Composition In Blue* was published in The Best American Short Plays 2013-2014.

CHARACTERS

Marty, male, late 20's, eager, romantic type, wears shiny shoes

Angie, female, mid 20's, sweet, Gracie Allen type

> *At rise, Marty and Angie are cuddled next to each other seated at a table by the window of a rooftop restaurant overlooking Times Square. It is New Years Eve, 1942. They look out the window at the celebration below.*

Marty: Well, here we are. Best seats in the house.

Angie: Best seats in the house.

Marty: Quite a view, hey?

Angie: Quite a view.

Marty: You look lovely. I like the hat.

Angie: Really? You don't think it's too fussy?

Marty: No, it suits you. I mean, it's very flattering on you.

Angie: Mmm. How did we get this table anyways?

Marty: I have connections.

Angie: Oooh.

Marty: Are you cold honey?

Angie: No, I'm fine. You?

Marty: This is a real swanky place. I feel like a fish out of water.

Angie: I wonder. Do you think fish mate for life?

Marty: What do you mean?

Angie: Don't you ever imagine what it's like, for you know, other species, the animals and birds and fish? I mean, how do they know what to do, what comes next?

Marty: It's all instinct, baby.

Angie: Because I've heard that certain species, certain ones do, that they actually mate for life.

Marty: Really?

Angie: Yes, it's true.

Marty: Fascinating.

Angie: And, as a matter of fact, you know my cousin, Paulie?

Marty: The guy who sold me this suit?

Angie: Right. That's right, I forgot about that. Well you know how he used to like to go hunting?

Marty: Uh huh.

Angie: And do you know why he quit hunting?

Marty: Haven't a clue.

Angie: Uncle Mike got so angry when Paulie told him he wouldn't hunt anymore on account of geese.

Marty: Geese?

Angie: Yeah. Because he heard, you know, that they mate for life.

Marty: You have a very unusual family.

Angie: Goodness, what time is it?

Marty: Look, the ball is coming down!

Angie: Our first New Year's Eve.

Marty: Kiss me.

> *They kiss.*

Angie: Mmm. Your kisses are sweet, like kosher wine.

> *She smacks her lips.*

Marty: What do you know from kosher wine?

Angie: I know enough to know it's sweet. And I know that it doesn't go with that Lobster Newburg you're eating.

Marty: Oops. *(Laughs.)* That'll be our little secret.

Angie: It's not as if a certain fella who professes to love a certain sweetheart would ever have her over for a Friday night dinner.

Marty: *Shabbos* dinner.

Angie: *Shabbos* dinner. See? I'm learning.

Marty: So you think my kisses are sweeter than kosher wine, hey?

Angie: Mmm hmm.

Marty: Don't tell your mother.

Angie: There's a lot I can't tell her about now.

She giggles.

Marty: Did you get what you wanted for Christmas?

Angie: Uh huh.

Marty: Everything?

Angie: Well, not EH-verything.

Marty: Have you been naughty?

Angie: Do you think I'm naughty?

Marty: I think you're nice.

Angie: What did your mother tell you about Catholic girls?

Marty: That they're nice. What did your mother tell you about Jewish boys?

Angie: That they're naughty.

They laugh.

Marty: No, really. I can imagine what she's thinking. She gives me this funny look every time I come over to pick you up.

Angie: At least I've had you over the house to meet my folks. That's more than I can say for you. Do you ever plan to take me home to meet your mother?

Marty: Come on, tell me. What does your mother say about me?

Angie: She thinks you're a good dresser. And she likes your shoes. She likes that they're always shiny.

Marty: Let's get married.

Angie: What?

> *From the crowd below in Times Square, we hear the celebrators shout, "Happy New Year! Happy New Year!"*

Marty: Geez, it's getting loud in here. Want to go somewhere else?

Angie: What did you say?

Marty: I said let's go somewhere else.

> *He rises.*

Angie: No, what you said before, did I want to…

Marty: I was going to ask you, *(He sits down.)* Wait, first I have a little surprise. *(He points out the window.)* See the theater across the street?

Angie: The Paramount?

Marty: That's the one. Can you read the marquis?

Angie: *(Reading.)* Appearing On Stage Tonight, The Benny Goodman Orchestra with Extra Added Attraction, Frank Sinatra. *(Excitedly.)* Oh Marty, you got us tickets to see Frank Sinatra?!

Marty: Not exactly. But I know a guy who knows a guy whose brother plays in Goodman's orchestra. He said come backstage after midnight and he'll see if he can get us in. We should get going in a few minutes. That is, if you want to see the show.

Angie: Do I want to see the show? Wow. When you said you had connections, I thought…

Marty: That I was with the Jewish mafia? You think like we all know each other? No way. This is completely on the level. In fact, the guy I know, he's a *paisan*. He's married to my cousin so I guess that makes me a *paisan* too.

Angie: Really, you think so?

Marty: Really, I know so.

Angie: Gee Marty, that's swell.

Marty: Know what, they have a house out in the country and I've got an open invitation to visit whenever I want. I'll take you some time. You'd like it there.

Angie: Oh, I'd love to have a house in the country. A white house with green trim and a lilac bush, and a little yard in the back…

Marty: Angie…

Angie: …and a modern kitchen, and a different wallpaper pattern in each room…

Marty: I wanted to ask you…

Angie: …and an upstairs bedroom…

Marty: Do you want to get married?

Angie: What?

Marty: Married. Do you want to get married?

Angie: Are you asking me or are you <u>asking</u> me?

Marty: I'm <u>asking</u> you.

Angie: Well gee, what brought this on all of a sudden? I mean we haven't even…

Marty: I've been wanting to talk to you about it; could you maybe consider…

Angie: …and with the war and everything, do you think it's a good idea, I mean, what if…

Marty: Exactly. What if? What if I get called? What if I have to go over, will you wait for me?

Angie: I, I don't… you know my friend Patty? Her fiancé just got called up. She got so hysterical, they had to give her a sedative. I felt so bad for her and all. But you know, the thing is, I was glad it wasn't me, <u>us</u>.

Marty: You can't put your head in the sand or just wish it would go away. You can bet I'll be called, that is, if I don't join up first.

Angie: Marty, no!

Marty: I'll tell you something that scares me. I had a dream the other night and I woke up in a sweat.

Angie: I don't think I want to hear this.

Marty: It was odd because I wasn't actually in the dream, but it was plain as day something bad had happened to me. I see my mother reading a letter, and then she clutches her chest and falls to the floor. Then, there were people sobbing, shoveling dirt, and they all huddled together, praying. Off in the distance, there was a figure, a woman shrouded in black. I couldn't make out a face but she looked sad, so sad, standing there alone.

Angie: Who do you think it was?

Marty: It was, I don't know, I think it was you. And that's the strange part. I wasn't so much upset about my fate, but more like, how this would be for Mama, and for you. *(Pause.)* I woke up thinking, what if something happened to me? What if my mother gets that letter and she's all alone with no one to comfort her? What if you had to bear it alone?

Angie: And that's why you want to marry me?

Marty: Ange, there never was any question in my mind that I would marry you. I knew it from the moment we met. It's just that there were certain things I had to work out in my mind, certain differences we had to smooth over.

Angie: Like chalk and cheese.

Marty: Chalk and cheese?

Angie: Uh huh. You said we were like chalk and cheese, oil and water, apples and oranges.

Marty: I said that?

Angie: Yes, that's exactly what you said.

Marty: I guess I was trying to be clever. But you knew what I was talking about, didn't you?

Angie: You know, Marty, you think we're so different from each other, like with the religion and the family background and all. But it turns out we're more alike than we thought.

Marty: That's what I've been trying to tell you.

Angie: I mean we like the same music and movies…

Marty: So like I've been saying…

Angie: …and we like to go dancing and driving in the country and…

Marty: …which is why I wanted to…

Angie: …and we're close to our families, I mean we're practically family already, right *paisan*?

Marty: Right, *paisan*. Speaking of, do you still want to go over to the Paramount and get a peak at Frankie?

Angie: You and me and about a zillion bobby soxers? I don't know. I kind of like being here with you.

Marty: Wait a minute, wait a minute. I've got a better idea. Grab your hat.

Angie: Where are we going?

Marty: Penn Station. I think we can catch the one fifteen train.

Angie: Where to?

Marty: Elkton, Maryland!

> *Marty reaches in his pocket, pulls out some cash and plunks it down on the table. For a brief second, they both stare at each other in bewildered anticipation. Marty takes Angie by the hand and in a burst of excitement, they rush toward the exit.*

<u>End of play.</u>

On the Move

By

Michael C. Buss

On the Move was first produced in Orange County in December, 1998, directed by the playwright.

Michael Buss is a playwright/actor/software developer and lives in Santa Ana, Southern California. He was the second President of New Voices Playwrights Workshop, of which he is a founder member. Being originally English, a sly Pythonesque edge often creeps into his text.

Michael Buss's short plays have nearly all been produced in Southern California: The Theatre District, CA; The Chance Theater, CA; Stages, CA; The Vanguard, CA; Cabrillo Playhouse, CA; Costa Mesa Playhouse, CA; Stage Door Repertory Playhouse, CA; The Gallery Theatre, CA; Empire Theater, CA; Newport Theatre Arts Center, CA. He has also had a full length workshop productions at South Coast Repertory Theater, Stages, and Stage Door Repertory Theatre.

Readers wishing to see more of Michael's plays may visit http://mbuss.com/plays.php

CHARACTERS

Barbara Thomason, female, 35-45, well educated.

Mister Clough, (pronounced Cluff), 45-50.

Mister Farthingdale, 45-50.

Clough and Farthingdale are movers who, despite being dressed for the job, have a bearing of dignity and propriety. They are serious in the bland, innocent fashion of those for whom honesty is the only code they have ever known.

> *The present. The bedroom of Barbara's apartment. The bed is center stage, with the foot to the audience. There is an imaginary wall at the front of the stage, with an equally imaginary but very tangible doorway two thirds of the way across. The longer part of the wall, within the bedroom, is where the wardrobe would be. A window (also imaginary) is to the side, opposite the doorway. NOTE: Wherever a forward slash '/' is inserted in a speech, at that very point the next speech begins. AT RISE. Music is a slow moody melody from a double bass. The lights build to reveal Barbara pacing restlessly round the room, checking her watch. She hears a truck pulling up and goes to the window. The movers have arrived. Barbara leans out of the window, looks down and waves.*

Barbara: Hello! I'm up here. Hello! Yes, up here. Come on in. Door's open. Just come on up. *(Paces round some more.)* About time, too; never can rely on these men. I always used to say, "If you want something done, do it

yourself." But this is when you actually need a man!
God, if I don't get out of here by 3 he'll be back. Come
on, hurry up.

> *A beat, then enter CLOUGH and
> FARTHINGDALE. They walk across the front of
> the stage from the window side appearing to
> notice something in the wall before they reach
> the doorway. This is mimed. Timidly they enter
> the room and then the characters 'see' each
> other.*

Oh, there you are. Come on in.

Clough: Well, here we are. And we are in.

Barbara: Good. What kept you? I was expecting you
half an hour ago.

Clough: Well, we had a little meeting, you might call
it. Got held up.

Farthingdale: Yeah, sort of ran into someone on the
way. We, er, hadn't met before, though.

Barbara: Never mind, we have work to do.

Farthingdale: Only we might not ever meet him again.

Barbara: Look, this really has nothing to do with me.

Clough: Except we might not ever meet him again.

Barbara: Really. Interesting. As if I really minded at
all.

Clough: We just ran into him, you see.

Barbara: Yes, I believe I do see. Very well. But that's your business, not mine. So if you don't mind let's just get on with moving the bed?

Clough: *(Checking details from a work sheet on clip board.)* Says here "One small item of furniture - Unspecified." Right. So... you want us to move the bed?

Barbara: Yes. The bed. That's what I told the clerk at your company. *(Speaking very deliberately.)* I want this bed taken out of this apartment and delivered to another apartment. If I could use shorter words, I would. Should I say it louder?

Clough: We can't do that.

Barbara: For Chrissake, why not? You're movers, aren't you? I saw what it said on the side of your truck.*(Strides over to look out of window.)* "We move you. Anything, any time, any distance." So here I am, this is my bed, the time is now, and I need this out.

Farthingdale: Beg pardon Ma'am. Not wishing to be rude. And we didn't mean to contradict the sign on the side of the truck, but the fact is, that bed won't go through this door. Therefore we can't move it.

Clough: I second that.

Barbara: This is ridiculous. I've never heard anything so stupid in all my life. How, please tell me, do you suppose it got <u>in</u> here in the first place?

Clough: Through the door.

Barbara: Then if it came in through the door, please take it out through the door.

Farthingdale: Ma'am.

Barbara: Yes?

Farthingdale: It was, er, a different door.

Barbara: *(Stunned.)* Excuse me? There is only one door. How could it be a different door?

Clough: What Mr. Farthingdale means...

Barbara: What did you call him?

Clough: Mister Farthingdale.

Barbara: Why this Mister So-and-So? I thought all you guys were called Bill, or Steve, or Kevin, or something. I never even thought of you as Mister anybody.

Farthingdale: That's exactly it. We are of the old school. And we don't like being treated just like /movers.

Clough: Movers, moving men.

Farthingdale: We don't like being looked down on so we dignify our profession by using our full names.

Barbara: I see. That's very admirable. And what did you say your name was?

Clough: I didn't. But since you ask, it's Clough. Mister Clough.

Barbara: Right. Mister Clough and Mister Farthington.

Farthingdale: *(Correcting her.)* Dale.

Barbara: What?

Farthingdale: Dale. It's Farthingdale, not Farthington. A lot of people get that wrong.

Barbara: Look, I don't care whether I got it right or wrong. What about this door? Just take my bed through it. Okay?

Clough: Like we were saying, it's a different door from the one it came in through.

Farthingdale: Yeah. Mr. Clough and I noticed on the way in. He says, look, they've moved that door. Didn't do a very good job of it, did they? And I said, that could mean trouble if she's got a bed or anything big to move.

Barbara: But why? You've lost me.

Clough: Look, when the doorway was over here *(Indicating.)* there was plenty of room to swing big furniture round into the hallway. But now the room has been re-modeled, and the doorway is here, there is almost no room to maneuver. This was done by some enthusiast who had nothing better to do with his spare time but wander round Home Depot wondering what he can "improve" next. So the bed - which no doubt came in through that door, which now isn't a door - will almost certainly not go out of this door...

Farthingdale: ...which <u>is</u> a door.

Clough: Thank you Mr. Farthington.

Farthingdale: Dale.

Clough: Sorry! See, Miss, even I get it wrong
sometimes.

Barbara: I am not a Miss.

Clough: Ma'am.

Barbara: That'll do. I still prefer Mrs. Thomason.

Clough: Uh-oh! That's peculiar... /that was the name
of...

Barbara: There's nothing peculiar about it at all. A
perfectly good name.

Clough: Yes, Mrs. Thomason. You did say Thomason?

Barbara: I did. Your hearing appears to be impeccable.
And for your information my husband was the one who,
as you put it, had nothing better to do with his time but
wander round Home Depot. He re-modeled the room to
make space for the wardrobe. And then... guess what?
We went out and bought a bed. Yes, in case you
wonder, this bed. And, if I might be so bold as to add to
what should be your considerable discomfiture...

Clough: Good word. Very good. You don't hear that
one every day.

Barbara: *(Continuing from the interruption.)* ...your
discomfiture, the bed came in through that door! It took
some doing. Almost didn't make it. But we did it.
Albert and I.

Farthingdale: Albert? Did you say Albert?

Barbara: Yes. And now the stinking son of a bitch is leaving me.

Farthingdale: That's funny. Only two hours ago...

Barbara: It is not funny. I am very unamused and it is time to move.

> *Clough has been checking over the door and, by eye, sizing up the problem with rather exaggerated 'tut-tuts' and shaking of the head, etc.*

Clough: Mister Farthingdale, I reckon the lady's right.

Barbara: Of course I am right, you, you... Geez!

Farthingdale: But we still can't move the bed.

Barbara: *(Pause.)* I guess this is where I should act surprised and become hysterical. But you know what? I won't. I am beginning to resign myself to a dreadful fate. I feel it coming. So I will retreat to my bed, even as I speak, and ask you in earnest tones and grave, WELL WHY THE HELL NOT?

Clough: *(Looking surprised.)* We normally leave it to our clients to remove the bedding first.

Barbara: Oh. How thoughtless of me. I am so sorry. It simply never crossed my mind. I guess, with paying you, as I am - though at this rate I might not - I supposed you might just do it for me. You, I take it, have big black plastic bags to put things in.

Farthingdale: /Yes but we're both...

Clough: The trouble is that we... (*Pause.*)

Farthingdale: After you, Mr. Clough

Clough: We are both allergic, you see.

Barbara: To what?

Clough: (*Hesitates.*) Bed bugs!

Barbara: (*Leaping up in rage.*) I do not have bed bugs! How dare you even suggest it. I am going right away to phone your company /and...

Farthingdale: He meant bed mites. House dust mites. They're everywhere. But specially in beds. Sorry Miss, er Ma'am. We didn't mean to be rude.

Clough: Yes. House dust mites. Sorry. Sorry.

Barbara: (*Eyes them suspiciously.*) Both of you?

Clough: Yes, both of us.

Farthingdale: (*They both nod.*) Allergic.

Barbara: All right then. I accept your apology. But, I'm taking five bucks off the invoice for this.

Farthingdale: That's fine. That's just fine. But we have another problem.

> *She now breathes very deeply and sets off on a long slow walk around the bedroom. The men make way for her and watch her with great apprehension.*

Barbara: I wonder if we might, perhaps, have a little rehearsal of where we're at. If necessary I will make coffee for you. I'll stir in the sugar until it is all dissolved and you cannot feel the gritty bits on the bottom.

Farthingdale: On the bottom.

Barbara: The gritty bits, on the bottom. And I promise to speak with great calm and treat you with the dignity that befits men of your noble profession.

Clough: Sounds good to me.

> *They all sit on the bed, Barbara up by the pillows, the men at the foot of the bed.*

Barbara: I have a problem. I realize you probably don't care about my problem, seeing I don't give a rat's ass about yours. Nonetheless...

Clough: You're going to tell us!

Barbara: Yes! I am.

Farthingdale: We're very good listeners.

> *The men react suitably to this speech. They make out to be attentive, understanding and deeply caring.*

Barbara: Fine! I have been unhappy for a long time. In fact it really goes back to the time Albert moved the door and we bought the bed. This was meant to be the solution to all our problems. Do you understand?

> *They shake their heads.*

Barbara: Things were not going, or had not been going well... *(She gestures at the bed.)*

Clough: Between the /sheets!

Farthingdale: In bed!

Barbara: Yes. So we got counseling and found out that if we invested more time in making the evenings, the nights, if you wish, more relaxed and enjoyable, things might improve. I ordered new curtains, a new wardrobe, Albert moved the door to make space for it, we redecorated the whole room and then we chose this bed.

Farthingdale: Good choice. Very nice bed.

Barbara: I agree. But, I might as well tell you, things didn't improve. They went from bad to worse.

Clough: You don't mean... ?

Barbara: Yes, I do.

Farthingdale: You poor woman.

Barbara: I know. It was dreadful.

Farthingdale: But how could you... ?

Barbara: I don't know. But I did.

Clough: I am so /sorry.

Farthingdale: We both /are.

Barbara: No. You don't have to be. Because, you see, now I am glad. Albert, whom I used to adore...

Farthingdale: Until he moved it.

Clough: Moved what?

Barbara: The door. "Whom I used to adore?" It was a joke Mr. Clough.

Clough: *(This one has escaped him!)* Oh!

Barbara: The aforementioned Albert became a bore. He channeled himself into his work. He would always have to read just a few more reports or write a few more checks. Or if the TV was on there was just one more inning, or he had to see who knocked out who. Anything. Any old excuse to avoid… And so, I lost interest. It didn't happen overnight - well it never did, that was the problem - but over a period of several months I just got used to being on my own. So one day I made the big decision. I said, Barbara my dear,

Clough: Is that your name, then?

Barbara: Yes, Mister Clough. You're getting sharper, I can see. I said, Barbara my dear, it is time for a change. He clearly doesn't need me. He can learn to live alone. He can keep everything in the house. I don't care. I have far more money than him. But not the bed. I will keep the bed. I will find new ways to put it to good use. So I'm leaving and, with your help, taking the bed with me. That, gentlemen, is where I need your help. I need it urgently, like I need it NOW! So if I fold up the bedding, please, if it's not too much trouble, will you two kindly stir yourselves to move the friggin' bed.

> *The men look astonished at the language! Then*
> *Farthingdale rises and stands addressing the*
> *other two, both still on the bed.*

Farthingdale: If I may, I also would like to embark
upon a brief, shall we say, disquisition?

> *They speak simultaneously*

Clough: Disquisition.

Barbara: Disquisition.

Farthingdale: Disquisition. Did everybody used to
watch Naked Gun? No matter. We have now
ascertained that, albeit with some difficulty, this bed
can in fact be twisted and maneuvered out of the door
since, amazingly, it came in through it. And we have
the agreement, for a 5 dollar discount on the final
invoice, tax being due on the discounted not the original
amount, that Mrs. Barbara...

Barbara: I like that. Mrs. Barbara. Yes. Nice.

Farthingdale: Yes, that Ma'am here will fold up the
bedding.

> *The others all nod.*

However, there is one remaining issue.

> *He hooks his thumbs in the straps of his*
> *overalls. Barbara gazes profoundly at the*
> *ceiling with lips pursed, breathing out a slow*
> *but fierce hiss.*

Barbara: Of course. There would have to be. Even old prunes dying of cancer go into remission and have one last kick. And believe me you are going to die unless the bed is moved. This had better be the very last kick.

Farthingdale: Yes ma'am. Well, I have to explain that I am a tops man but he, Mister Clough, is into bottoms.

Barbara: *(In total disbelief.)* Oh. Is that so?

Clough: I always do the bottoms.

Barbara: *(Shifting as far away from Clough as she can.)* Tell me, Mr. Clough. What exactly does this mean?

Clough: You were the one that first mentioned bottoms; gritty bits on the bottom, if I remember rightly.

Barbara: I was referring to sugar in the cup!

Farthingdale: Yes. Well we mean the bottom of furniture.

Clough: See, when you go up or down stairs with a large piece of furniture, someone has to take the top and someone takes the bottom. That's me. My back can't take the bending you get at the top, but I can do straight lifting. His back, Mister Farthingdale's back, can bend like a steel cable. He's like an ox. So he does the tops. All movers are like this. They work in pairs. One does tops and one does... bottoms. See?

Barbara: I see. But I don't see. Where's the problem?

Farthingdale: The point is he lost a contact lens on the way here, and he can't see his feet properly.

Barbara: So?

Farthingdale: Well we have to work to very strict health and safety regulations and if you can't see where you're putting your feet, especially on staircases, then that's a potential hazard, and if he falls, or even causes me to fall because he can't see his footing, and furthermore if it was avoidable because he could see he couldn't see and then still worked as though he could see, we wouldn't be covered by insurance, you see?

Barbara: You know? All of a sudden all the problems in the world now seem to pale by comparison. Crystal sunlight has come flooding into my poor benighted soul with a clarity that has flushed out all remaining shades of uncertainty. I am on angel wings. Nothing can touch me. In this one mad afternoon of total and utter frustration I have, as by magic, learned that anger and willpower accomplish nothing when the odds are so stacked against you that there is nothing to be done. I have attained a higher level of spiritual enlightenment in this short fifteen minutes than I ever thought would be possible in all the years I took Yoga classes. And I owe it all to you, Messrs. Clough and Farthingdale.

> *They clap this speech.*

May I ask you one final word of advice as to what I should now do? Not, I ask you to believe me, that I really care. I don't. Nothing matters. This is just idle curiosity.

Farthingdale: Anything to help, Ma'am.

Barbara: What do I now do about my husband? He'll be here in twenty minutes. I am now very happy. I would like to stay that way. But if I and my bed are still here when he returns I have this fear that having flown so close to the sun my wings may be made of wax and I shall fall headlong into a hell of despair. Gentlemen, you've got to help me! And if you're still here, you won't want to see him any more than I.

Farthingdale: *(Rising to the occasion again.)* A-hem! I, er, we, think we might be able to help you.

Barbara: Really? I can hardly wait to hear. Eighteen minutes left!

Clough: Well; Mr. Thomason, Albert, I think is the name of your, um, spouse?

Barbara: Yes.

Clough: Weighs about 230 pounds, slightly balding, dark, wearing kind of a tweed suit?

Barbara: Exactly.

Farthingdale: Often goes in the Habana for a beer and sandwich at lunchtime?

The men look at each other.

Barbara: Yes?

Clough: Well...

Farthingdale: He's not coming /home.

Clough: That's right. He's not coming home.

Barbara: How do you know?

Farthingdale: Well, like, we met him this afternoon.

Clough: Just bumped into him.

Farthingdale: That's why we were late. We tried to tell you.

Barbara: When?

Clough: When we got here. But you weren't interested.

Barbara: You met him? Did he tell you? Has he beaten me to the punch - he's leaving ME? My wings are melting!

Clough: He didn't really say very much.

Barbara: Well what did he say?

Clough: It was a sort of groan.

Barbara: You said you 'bumped' into him. Were you... in your truck... at the time?

Farthingdale: Like I said, we ran into someone. That's why we were late. The police had a lot of questions.

Clough: We ran him over. He's, er, not coming home.

> *They stand in embarrassed silence. Barbara sinks on to the bed with head in hands, her shoulders shaking with contained emotion.*

Farthingdale: We are... very sorry Ma'am. It, er, was an accident. He just came out of the pub as we were passing and... didn't stop to look. There was no time...

Clough: ...to stop.

Farthingdale: We have to go now. The police need to see us again. I guess, we may as well leave the bed where it is?

Clough: Under the circumstances, why don't you pay half the invoice? You know, call out fee. Less, 5 dollars.

Barbara: *(Raising her head from her hands.)* To be precise, Albert is dead!

Clough: Yes. Like I said, it was an accid...

Barbara: You killed him, with your truck!

Farthingdale: Yes.

Clough: We are very /sorry.

Farthingdale: We are very, very sorry.

Barbara: Are you? Good. Well, no, I suppose you needn't be. *(She begins to laugh, almost hysterically.)* Mr. Farthingdale and Mr. Clough. Think of it. In a brief period of one day of my tedious, humdrum existence you have not only delivered me from the bane of my life, but you have pushed me through humiliation and frustration into a new serenity and freedom. I've spent time on my bed with two strange men and they've made me laugh. I owe you guys. I owe you. So I will pay your invoice, all of it, though you never moved the bed one inch!

Clough: Less 5 bucks?

Barbara: Idiots!

She throws pillows at them. Blackout.

End of play.

The Scarf

By

Linda Whitmore

Linda Whitmore is a playwright and screenwriter living in Southern California. She is a founding member of New Voices Playwrights Theatre & Workshop. Her plays have been produced at Stages Theatre, CA; Chance Theater, CA; Cabrillo Playhouse, CA; Costa Mesa Playhouse, CA; Vanguard Theatre, CA; Garden Grove Playhouse, CA; Gallery Theatre, CA; Empire Theatre, CA; Mysterium Theater, CA; and Stage Door Rep, CA.

CHARACTERS

Charlotte, female, 50s or 60s

Jean, female, 50s or 60s

> *A middle class, suburban living room. The present. At rise, Jean is in the living room, applying lip gloss. The doorbell rings.*

Jean: Coming!

> *Jean tucks the lip gloss into her purse and rushes to the door and opens it. Charlotte enters, carrying a small gift bag from which colorful, decorative tissue blooms. They hug. Air kisses.*

Charlotte: Jean!

Jean: Charlotte! It's been too long!

Charlotte: I know! Happy birthday!

Jean: You look great!

Charlotte: So do you!

Jean: Come on in.

> *They walk to the sofa and sit. Charlotte puts the gift bag on the coffee table.*

Charlotte: It's great that our schedules finally let us have one afternoon when we're not being pulled in every direction by husbands...

Jean: And kids!

Charlotte: Them, too! And my job. God, my job.

Jean: My church group takes almost all of my free time.

Charlotte: Got you a little something.

Jean: You shouldn't have! You said you'd pay for lunch; that's more than generous.

Charlotte: I saw it and thought of you. Do you want to open it now or at the restaurant?

Jean: Now, I think. I don't want the waiters to see it's my birthday and sing "Happy Birthday." God. Embarrassing.

Charlotte: That's true.

> *Charlotte hands Jean the gift bag. Jean extricates a box from the bag and opens it. She unfolds more tissue and removes a gauzy scarf with symbols on it.*

Jean: Oh, Charlotte! It's gorgeous! Thank you!

> *They hug awkwardly on the sofa.*

Charlotte: You're so welcome! I thought, in that color, you could wear it with almost anything.

> *Jean unfurls the scarf and walks to a mirror on the wall. She admires it and starts to wrap it around her neck. Suddenly, something catches her eye.*

Jean: What's this?

Charlotte: What's what?

Charlotte crosses to Jean to examine the scarf.

Jean: There's… Are these letters?

Charlotte: Let me see. I really didn't notice.

Jean: It looks like writing. Where did you buy this?

Charlotte: Cost Plus World Market. The return receipt is in the box if you want a different color.

Jean: Where was this made?

Jean searches for a tag.

Pakistan.

Charlotte: So what?

Jean: So what? So they chop off people's heads!

Charlotte: No they don't! Isn't that, like, Saudi Arabia?

Jean: They do it in Saudi Arabia, too. They're savages. All of them. I can't wear this. What if someone from my church sees me?

Charlotte: Do you really think it would be a problem?

Jean: Yes! Look at this "worm writing" …

Charlotte: "Worm writing"?

Jean: Worm writing! Worm writing! It's what all those people over there use!

Charlotte: "Those people"?

Jean: You know what I mean. Muslims. I'm a Christian woman. This is a Christian country!

Charlotte: Well, it was founded on Christian principals.

Jean: I don't expect you to understand. Because… you know.

Charlotte: Because I'm Jewish?

Jean: You know that has nothing to do with this. I just wish… I just wish this country could be the way it was when I was growing up.

Charlotte: Jean, when you were growing up, blacks were marching for civil rights, abortion was illegal and the Americans and Soviets were trying to blow up the world.

Jean: Just how old do you think I am?

Charlotte: A year older than you were yesterday.

Jean: Well, I look back on how bad things were when I was young, and I think, wow, that was pretty bad. But look at things now, and every day people are blowing themselves up with suicide bombs, chopping off people's heads; they kidnap girls and sell them to old men!

Charlotte: It's just extremists who do that, Jean. It's small factions of people who do that. They're sick...

Jean: No! Sick is when you get cancer! They're evil. No one uses that word anymore... evil. It's not in the American lexicon anymore. Well, I, for one, believe in good, old-fashioned evil. You know what my theory is? That back in the 1960s, when we were growing up, people started to major in psychology in college. And suddenly, people thought they could figure out why one person kills another person. They said it was because the murderers were "sick." They were abused as children. Or they heard voices in their head. Or the only way they could get sexual satisfaction was by killing someone. Well I think everyone has a dark side. I know when someone cuts me off on the freeway and I honk, I've given in a little to that dark side. Or if someone steals my parking place at the grocery store and I give them the stink-eye, that's giving in just a little to that dark side. But I don't run people off the road. Or shoot them or blow them up. The entire pillar of civilized society depends on John Doe or Jane Doe *not* giving in to their base instincts. Or there'd be chaos in the streets. And you know what? Those people in the Middle East, they're the exact opposite of that. They band together and they plan murder and mayhem. They *plan* it! They are remorseless. They think God is on their side. How the hell does beheading people and putting the video on the Internet win people over to your cause?

Charlotte: I don't think they're trying to win people over to their cause.

Jean: Then why do it? Why cause suffering?

Charlotte: Look, I can't walk a mile in their shoes. So I don't know. And you can't walk a mile in their shoes, either.

Jean: It's a different world from when we were growing up, all right. A much, much worse one.

Charlotte: Jean, I didn't notice the writing on the scarf. I thought they were decorative symbols.

> *Charlotte gathers the scarf and begins to put it back in the box.*

I'll exchange it. I'm sorry if it offended you.

Jean: I'm sorry, Charlotte.

> *Charlotte picks up her purse.*

Charlotte: I'm afraid I've lost my appetite. I don't think I'd be very good company right now.

Jean: Please don't leave like this.

Charlotte: I'm sorry, Jean… I'll exchange the scarf and mail it to you.

> *Charlotte reluctantly exits carrying the gift bag. Jean looks longingly at the front door. Then Jean goes to her purse, removes lip gloss and starts to apply it. The doorbell rings.*

Jean: It's open!

> *Charlotte enters, carrying a small gift bag from which colorful, decorative tissue blooms. They hug. Air kisses.*

Jean: Charlotte! It's been too long!

Charlotte: I know! Happy happy!

Jean: Thanks! You look great!

Charlotte: So do you, Jean!

Jean: Come on in!

> *The two walk to the sofa and sit. Charlotte parks the gift bag on the coffee table.*

The Scarf

Charlotte: It's great that our schedules finally let us
have one afternoon when we're not being pulled in all
directions by husbands...

Jean: ...and my job. God my job!

Charlotte: Between my kids and my church group, I
don't have time to think!

> *Charlotte parks the gift bag on the coffee table.*

Jean: You shouldn't have!

Charlotte: Nonsense. Open it! I hope you like it.

> *Charlotte hands Jean the gift bag. Jean
> extricates a box from the bag and opens it. She
> unfurls more tissue and removes a gauzy scarf
> with symbols on it.*

Jean: Oh, Charlotte! It's gorgeous! Thank you!

> *They hug awkwardly on the sofa.*

Charlotte: You're so welcome! I thought, in that color
you could wear it with almost anything.

> *Jean unfurls the scarf and walks to a mirror on
> the wall. She admires it and starts to wrap it
> around her neck.*

Jean: You have such great taste in clothes.

> *Jean turns to Charlotte.*

How do I look?

Charlotte: I was right; great color with your hair…
Wait. What's that?

Jean: What's what?

> *Charlotte crosses to Jean and holds up part of the scarf.*

Charlotte: Oh my God. That looks like Arabic writing!

Jean: It does? Looks like decorations to me.

Charlotte: Where was this made?

> *Charlotte grabs the scarf to look for a tag, choking Jean in the process.*

Jean: Wh... hrph...

Charlotte: Oh my God. Pakistan.

Jean: So what?

Charlotte: So what? They're Muslims! They fly planes into buildings!

Jean: Well. Not all Muslims. Or there wouldn't be any buildings left.

Charlotte: I should have looked at the scarf more closely before I bought it.

Jean: Charlotte, I love the scarf! What can I say?

Charlotte: What if this says "Praise Allah" or something!

Jean: What if it does?

Charlotte: You're Jewish. I won't let the terrorists win!

Charlotte tries to wrestle the scarf from around Jean's neck.

Jean: Wha...

Charlotte: I'm returning it!

Jean: You'll do no such thing! The terrorists will pry this scarf from my cold, dead fingers.

Charlotte: That's not funny!

Jean: I'm kidding, Charlotte. You know what? I love this scarf. I'm going to wear it loud and proud. In fact, I'm going to wear it to the restaurant!

Charlotte: What if someone from your synagogue sees us?

Jean: I can say with almost total certainty that none of the congregants speaks Arabic.

Charlotte: I couldn't live with myself if anything bad happened to you.

Jean: I have an idea.

Jean grabs her phone and surfs the Internet.

If anyone says something about the scarf... let's see, how do I say, "Fuck you" in Arabic?

Charlotte laughs.

C'mon. Let's go. I get to pick the restaurant because I'm the birthday girl! Feel like some Indian?

They exit.

<u>End of play.</u>

Tele-Toss: A Moving Experience

By

Lillian Nader

 Lillian Nader is a novelist/playwright/copyeditor living in Southern California. She has been published in the *New Voices Holiday Plays 2019* anthology available on Amazon and Lulu. She is the author of the play, *Blue Hair & Rap*, which was performed at the Stage Door Repertory Theatre in the Holiday Voices 2019 show. She is the author of *Theep and Thorpe: Adventures in Space*, a science fiction novel for young readers (2016) and a contributing author to *Muse & Ink: Soul Expressions Through Writing* by Heather Rivera (2019). Additional publications include educational workbooks on collaborative learning in the classroom. In addition to imaginative wordsmithing, Lillian is a freelance copyeditor of nonfiction and fiction books and stories. Her play, *Tele-Toss: A Moving Experience*, is an adaptation of a scene from her novel, *Theep and Thorpe: Adventures in Space*. Lillian is a retired special needs teacher with a background of teaching at a juvenile court school in Santa Ana, CA. and a Charter School for Troubled Youth. Her background in metaphysics influenced her creation of Theep & Thorpe, enlightened space beings on Planet Staruus, who can be seen only by kids. Lillian is thrilled to be the newest member of New Voices Playwrights as of September 6, 2019.

CHARACTERS

Dr. Weir, male, 30-40, school director, telepathy teacher

Jonathon, male, 14, troubled youth, can manifest objects

Hazel, female, 13, naturally telepathic

Travis, male, 12, can teleport objects

Billy, male 15, athletic, reformed bully

Theep, female space being, performed by a child

Thorpe, male space being, performed by a child

> *At rise, we are in the telepathy classroom of Dr. Weir and students Jonathon, Hazel, Travis, and Billy. Dr. Weir stands in front of the classroom to address the students seated in chairs. A large desk is at stage right.*

Dr. Weir: *(To students.)* I have an important announcement concerning each of you. We are implementing a competition with the telepathy teams under my direction. Training begins tonight.

Jonathon: What the heck?.

Dr. Weir: Hang on, Jonathon, all your questions will be answered soon. My idea is based on recent feedback from students here at the Planet Staruus Juvenile Court School who wish to participate in team sports.

Students mumble among themselves.

Quiet, please! The telepathy contest provides a unique opportunity for your team to compete while continuing to hone your telepathy skills. You're gonna love it!

Hazel: So how does this game work? This is my first day in telepathy class… I can't compete.

Dr. Weir: Do not worry, my dear. You and your partner, Travis, will have a few months to practice in class and during free time to become part of the strongest telepathy team. You'll catch on to it in no time. So, let's begin.

Dr. Weir holds up a set of cards and shows them to the students.

I've prepared some new images for you to practice sending to your partners. My other four classes will do the same.

Billy groans. Everyone talks at once.

Travis: What free time? We never have free time.

Jonathon: *(Scoffs.)* This isn't team sports!

Billy: I ain't no good at this stuff, Dr. Weir. I play basketball or soccer… not this brainy crap.

Hazel: Yeah, wouldn't basketball work better for us kids?

Dr. Weir: All right, let's get the discussion out of the way. The other teams have already excited about the idea, and we've come up with a solution to the free time concern. You can meet on nights you don't attend this class, and the others will meet on their free nights. Fair enough?

Travis: I guess so, but won't we be competing against each other? It doesn't make sense for us to practice together.

All mumble at once again.

Dr. Weir: *(Shakes his head.)* Now, you know we don't allow contact sports here at the juvenile school for obvious reasons.

Jonathon causes a basketball to manifest in his hands and another one to appear in Billy's hands. Then a hoop appears on the wall. Jonathon's ball moves toward the hoop, drops, and bounces back into his hands.

Billy: Yes! Now this is something I can get excited about!

Dr. Weir: Hold it right there! What just happened, Jonathon?

Jonathon: It's like I've been trying to tell you in our counseling sessions; these weird things just happen. I conjured up the balls, but I didn't make them move.

Travis: Hey, Dr. Weir, what if instead of telepathy cards, we spend our time learning to move basketballs with our minds? How about that idea?

The basketball in Billy's hands starts to move. Billy struggles to hold onto it. The ball

151

> *glides through the air to Hazel, who reaches
> out and catches it. The ball in Jonathon's
> hands moves across the room to Travis.*

Dr. Weir: Okay, Travis, you've made your point. It's becoming clear you students have talents I never knew about.

Jonathon: Hey, I didn't know Travis could do that!

Travis: Nobody knows. I don't want people thinking I'm a freak. But if more of us could do it, I wouldn't feel so alone.

> *The desk at stage right slides across the room
> with Theep and Thorpe seated on top.
> Everyone sees them except Dr. Weir.*

Dr. Weir: Oh, I see what you mean, Travis. You really do have an amazing gift!

Travis: But, Dr. Weir, I didn't move the desk.

Dr. Weir: *(Alarmed.)* What? That desk moved. We all saw it move!

Travis: Oh, I saw it move, Sir, but I'm not the one who moved it.

Dr. Weir: *(Losing it.)* Who moved that desk?

> *The students look toward Theep and Thorpe,
> seated on top of the desk.*

Theep: Hello, everyone. How's tricks?

Billy: Hello yourself. Where did you come from?

Dr. Weir: To whom are you speaking, Billy? Things are becoming confused enough without you talking to the furniture.

Hazel: *(Amused.)* So, Travis, do you think you can teach us to move stuff?

Travis: Sure, I can give it a try.

Dr. Weir: Oh, no you won't! Not until someone tells me how that desk moved across the room. I ask you again, Travis. Did you move that desk?

Travis: No, Sir, I can't move furniture… only basketballs… like this.

> *Travis teleports the basketball to Theep, who catches it. Hazel physically tosses her ball to Thorpe. Theep and Thorpe remain visible to all but Dr. Weir*

Dr. Weir: Hmm, this seems to be another skill I wasn't aware of… causing balls to hover in the air.

Jonathon: *(Chuckles.)* Raise your hand if you see two crazy looking creatures with triangular faces.

> *All but Dr. Weir raise their hands. Theep and Thorpe drop the balls simultaneously and bounce then up and down in sync.*

Dr. Weir: Jonathon, what kind of balls are these? They seem to have magical power.

> *Theep's ball rises toward the hoop and sinks a perfect basket. Thorpe passes his ball to Hazel. Hazel throws the ball and makes*

> *another basket. Billy retrieves the balls and tosses them to Theep and Thorpe. The "hovering balls" each sail in different directions and continue to be caught, bounced, and sunk into baskets.*

Okay, I get the idea that basketball is something you guys really want, but some modifications are needed. Jonathon, do you think you could make the balls a bit smaller?

Jonathon: Sure, I'll give it a try.

> *Jonathon closes his eyes. Lights dim to blackout and fade back up. Jonathon opens his eyes. He holds a container with several balls about the size of a softball with a spongy texture. Dr. Weir lifts one of the balls, inspects it, and tests it. He bounces it and tosses it across the room without doing any damage.*

Dr. Weir: All right, then. I can see the possibilities of this new game. We'll call it Tele-Toss, and you students will practice sending the balls back and forth. Just that. No fancy stuff. Agreed?

All: Yes!

Jonathon: Anything's better than those boring telepathy cards!

End of play.

Up in the Clouds

By

Mark Bowen

Up in the Clouds was first produced at Stage Door Repertory Theatre in June, 2019, directed by Geoffrey Gread and starring Jeremy Krasovic and Lily Edwards.

Mark Bowen is an actor, teacher, and playwright living in Southern California. His first play, *Not Something Else*, was produced at Long Beach City College, where he is a former member of the board of trustees. Since becoming a member of New Voices he has had many other one-acts produced in their annual Summer Voices Festival. His first full-length play, *Weeds of Sloth,* opened at Community Actors Theatre in San Diego in June of 2016.

<u>CHARACTERS</u>

Leonard, male, mid-late 20s, a doctor

Mia, female, early 20s, his patient

<u>Scene 1: Mia's Hospital Room.</u>

> *Mia is in the bed, asleep. Leonard is in a chair at the other end of the room.*

Leonard: *(Softly.)* I can't do this… I just…

> *He puts his face in his hands and then the phone rings. He goes to answer.*

Yes? *(Pause.)* Yeah, I told you I'll be right there.

> *He goes over to the bed, leans over and kisses Mia on the forehead. He then goes to the sink to get some water as Mia sits up in the bed.*

Okay. I can do this. I can… alright. *(Turns and sees Mia sitting up.)* Oh, I'm sorry. I hope you didn't hear me just now.

Mia: It's alright.

Leonard: Okay.

Mia: Is he here?

Leonard: Is who here?

Mia: You know who I'm talking about.

Leonard: Yeah. He's here.

Mia: So what are you waiting for?

Leonard: I just needed a moment. I'm sure you do, too.

Mia: What do you mean? I feel fine.

Leonard: Yeah, but your father. Seeing you like this.

Mia: *(Checking her wrists.)* They're all gone now.

Leonard: That wasn't me.

Mia: Oh?

Leonard: No. It's just that you won't see them. Not now.

Mia: Can't see the tattoo either.

Leonard: No, you shouldn't be able to see that anymore.

Mia: You sound so pleased.

Leonard: I'm sure your father would be. Your body as a "temple of the holy spirit"…

Mia: I didn't think you were religious.

Leonard: I'm not.

Mia: You know my father was an assistant pastor at our church, right?

Leonard: I think I remember hearing something like that.

Mia: You talked for a while last time?

Leonard: Not really.

Mia: *(Checking where the tattoo was.)* You know I got this back in High School? Got it just to piss him off?

Leonard: I figured something like that.

Mia: You know, he always expected me to be a doctor. Can you believe that?

Leonard: I can believe a lot about you, Mia.

Mia: Is that what you meant about your parents?

Leonard: What?

Mia: What you were saying to the other doctor… about how he reminded you of them.

Leonard: You were listening.

Mia: Yes. I'm sorry.

Leonard: Don't be.

Mia: I could have, you know.

Leonard: What?

Mia: Gone to medical school.

Leonard: Of course. I'm sure anything you'd set your mind to, you could have…

Mia: Oh, don't you start too!

Leonard: Alright.

Mia: My mind <u>was</u> set. Just not for what he… you know.

Leonard: Yeah.

Mia: He told you about the MCATs, right?

Leonard: Ninetieth percentile?

Mia: Ninety-second. *(Pause.)* So what did your parents expect out of you?

Leonard: What do you mean?

Mia: What was it that they wanted you to do? Instead of being a doctor?

Leonard: Is there anything else a parent would want?

Mia: But what you were saying about them being disappointed…

Leonard: That was gonna happen no matter what I did.

Mia: And yet you got to choose this.

Leonard: If that's what you want to call it.

There is a long silence.

Mia: So what was it?

Leonard: What was what?

Mia: What was it you really wanted, Doctor…

Leonard: Leonard.

Mia: Leonard… was there something else you wanted to do with your life?

Leonard: Does it matter?

Mia: Of course. It matters to me.

Leonard: Why? Why now?

Mia: I don't know. I just thought… right now I'd really like to know. I'm sure you had to have had something like that on your mind at the time.

Leonard: At the time?

Mia: Back in college. Right before you swallowed all your pills.

Leonard: You know.

Mia: Of course.

Leonard: Honestly… I have no idea what I wanted. Just not this. And this is why.

Mia: What? Me?

Leonard: Yes.

Mia: I'm ready if you are.

Leonard: You sure?

Mia: Yeah.

Leonard: Okay.

Mia: Your first time?

Leonard: Yeah.

Mia: You'll be fine. *(Pause.)* So, weren't you gonna tell me?

Leonard: Tell you what? I already told you, I never really knew what it was I wanted.

Mia: Not that. Not your career, just… you. Your life. What did you really want?

Leonard: Look, Mia…

Mia: No, tell me. When you were a kid, what did you really used to think about? You know, the kinds of things you give up on when you grow up.

Leonard: None of us ever really do that completely.

Mia: Leonard…

Leonard: You're not gonna let this go, are you?

Mia: No. And what do you have to lose? Not like it's ever leaving this room.

Leonard: True. Okay, look I don't really remember saying this, but…

Mia: Something your parents told you?

Leonard: My aunt.

Mia: You were too young to remember?

Leonard: Yes.

Mia: Yes! That's it. Tell me.

Leonard: I said I wanted to be up in the clouds.

Mia: Up in the clouds?

Leonard: I was walking with my aunt. She was talking about what a nice day it was. How pretty the clouds were up in the sky. I agreed, told her I wanted to be up there. And so she started to tell me about planes, what it'd be like when I got to take my first flight. And I said, "No, I want to <u>be</u> in the clouds"

Mia: *(Smiling.)* That wasn't so hard, now was it?

Leonard: It's stupid.

Mia: No, it's not.

Leonard: Look, it's just one of a million stupid things we all say when we're little. It didn't mean anything…

Mia: Sure it did, you wanted to…

Leonard: No, it wasn't that at all! Not about power, being a god, it's…

Mia: Yes. I understand.

Leonard: Funny thing is, now that I'm older…

Mia: Now that you're older, what?

Leonard: I guess now that kinda is what I really want.

Mia: What is?

Leonard: Power. *(Pause.)* No, not like that. Like… the power not to have to go through any of this.

Power to make things so nobody has to do this anymore, girls don't have to come in here to…

Long pause.

Mia: It's alright now, Leonard. None if it will matter anymore once you're up in those clouds.

Leonard: Don't do this, Mia.

Mia: That's not what I meant.

Leonard: I know. I'll go get your dad.

Mia: Leonard, wait! All I meant was… if it means anything to you, then I think you were right. You do deserve something better than this. I don't know if it makes things any easier for you, but I just wanted to say. What you said it was you wanted way back then, you deserve it.

Leonard: I was only a little boy, Mia.

Mia: Yes, I know. But it was you.

Leonard: Just try to get some rest now.

Mia: You do, Leonard. You deserve that, and so much more.

> *She kisses him. Then she lies back in the bed and is immediately asleep again. He follows her down, and kisses her again on the forehead, like before, then gets up and heads to the door as the lights go out.*

Scene 2: <u>The Waiting Room</u>

> *A single spot of light comes up on Leonard.*

Leonard: Mr. Robertson, thank you for getting here so quickly. Your daughter was admitted just after midnight. She had slashed her wrists again, and by the time we got her in here she had already last a lot more blood than the last time. Like before we tried to… *(Pauses, and collects himself.)* Mr. Robertson, I am so sorry.

End of play.